'I have never had any doubts about the fact that I love you, Ricco.'

Anna touche ... e
white tablecl ... y,
probably can ... I
feel, but los ... ie
unsure of *my* ... ıg
the trouble. I keep imagining all sorts of crazy things simply because I can't remember the past and what happened.'

'I do understand, Anna. I understand how confused you must feel, how unsure, but you need have no doubts about how I feel. I love you more than life itself, and never in any way would I set out to hurt you.'

Jennifer Taylor was born in Liverpool, England, and still lives in the north-west, several miles outside the city. Books have always been a passion of hers, so it seemed natural to choose a career in librarianship—a wise decision as the library was where she met her husband, Bill. Twenty years and two children later, they are still happily married, with the added bonus that she has discovered how challenging and enjoyable writing romantic fiction can be!

Recent titles by the same author:

TIDES OF LOVE
PLAYING AT LOVE

ENTICED

BY

JENNIFER TAYLOR

MILLS & BOON

All the characters in this book have no existence outside the imagination of the author, and have no relation whatsoever to anyone bearing the same name or names. They are not even distantly inspired by any individual known or unknown to the author, and all the incidents are pure invention.

*MILLS & BOON and the Rose Device are trademarks of the publisher.
Harlequin Mills & Boon Limited,
Eton House, 18–24 Paradise Road, Richmond, Surrey TW9 1SR*

ISBN 0 263 79584 5

*Set in 10½ on 12 pt Linotron Times
01-9608-49994*

*Typeset in Great Britain by CentraCet, Cambridge
Made and printed in Great Britain*

CHAPTER ONE

SHE lay so still in the bed, her face little darker than the starched white sheets drawn up to her chin. They had warned him that they had needed to shave her hair to operate but it was still a shock. His hands clenched slightly at his sides but his face remained expressionless. Riccardo Falcone had trained himself to hide his feelings and he hid them now. No one watching could have begun to guess at the torrent of emotions he felt right then as he remembered how it had felt to see the silken mass of her dark red hair spread across the pillows, to wrap it around his fingers. . .

The nurse at his side shifted slightly. He glanced at her, watching the colour come into her cheeks. She was uneasy in his company, probably wishing that someone would relieve her of this unwelcome task. How often had he seen that very same expression on other people's faces? He didn't even bother to work it out, unconcerned about how others viewed him.

'How long has she been here?'

The nurse jumped, her agitation more noticeable now. 'J-just over a week, Mr Falcone.'

'A week? Yet I was only informed this morning.' His deep, cold voice turned the statement into an accusation, his accent even more pronounced now, and the young woman looked away, wishing that the doctor would hurry up. She didn't want to remain here any longer than was necessary, yet she couldn't explain why she felt so on edge.

She shot a glance at the man as he turned back to stare through the plate glass window, studying him surreptitiously.

He was probably the most handsome man she had ever seen, with that jet-black hair, those blade-sharp features, but those startling silver eyes were ice-cold, his bearing so aloof that it set an immediate barrier between him and other people. She knew nothing about him apart from what she had read in the paper that morning, but, whoever Riccardo Falcone was, instinct told her that he wasn't a man to toy with, and she wished harder than ever that the doctor would come.

As though in answer to her prayers, Dr Lewis suddenly appeared. He dismissed her with a small nod, turning his attention immediately to the visitor as she hurriedly left the room.

'Mr Falcone, I'm Dr Lewis. We spoke earlier on the phone.'

Riccardo nodded. 'How badly injured is she?'

He made no attempt at small talk, his voice clipped, his face still expressionless, and the doctor suddenly understood why the nurse had looked at him with such relief. He cleared his throat, glancing at the clipboard he held, although he could recall each and every detail of his patient's progress.

'Physically your wife is recovering well from her injuries. Oh, there is still some painful bruising, a cracked rib which will continue to give her some discomfort for a while, but all that will heal. However, as I told you earlier, there does appear to be some problem with her memory.'

Riccardo turned away, walking to the small window which overlooked a bustling car park. The sky had that heavy grey look he always associated with England, the clouds swollen with rain. Back home the sun would be shining, the air would be sweet and clear. . .and the huge old house in Milan would be empty.

He swung round, a nerve ticking in his jaw, his silver eyes piercing as they focused on the older man. 'How badly affected is she? Does she remember anything at all?'

His voice grated and Dr Lewis cleared his throat again. 'Ehhmm, I know this is very difficult for you, Mr Falcone, but—'

He interrupted curtly, impatience glittering in the depths of the silver eyes which made such a startling contrast to his olive skin. 'I wish to know exactly how bad she is. Please do not try to spare my feelings, Doctor.'

'Very well, then. Your wife has no memory of the accident or anything which happened before it. She has no idea who she is, which is why it took so long to contact you. She wasn't carrying any identification at the time of the accident, nor was she reported missing. In fact, if it hadn't been for Nurse Shepherd spotting your photograph in the paper today, and recognising you from this, then we would still be completely in the dark as to her identity.'

He unclipped something from the board. Riccardo took it, feeling the shock like a physical blow. He turned back to the window, his hand clenching on the fragile paper as he struggled to control his emotions, but the photograph stared back at him like a silent accusation.

He turned it over and saw his own handwriting before the words blurred, but he didn't need to read them to recall what he had written. How long ago it seemed now, how many painful memories lay between then and now. If he could have just one wish then he would wish to turn back the clock and try again.

'All I can say, Mr Falcone, is that the mind is a delicate instrument. We don't understand a fraction of what can happen within it. Your wife's memory could return today, tomorrow or—'

'Or never.' Riccardo cut him off, not needing nor wanting to hear any more. 'I understand, Doctor. Now, if you will excuse me, I wish to be with my wife.'

He didn't wait for permission to be granted as he opened the door and walked into the small austere room, neither did he expect to be stopped as he closed the door behind him. What Riccardo Falcone wanted he got, what he chose to do he did—and no one had ever stopped him. Perhaps that was part of the trouble.

He stopped by the bed, looking down at the exquisite little face with its delicate features. Her hair was starting to grow back and there was a baby-fine fuzz of red-gold down all over her head.

Riccardo reached out and touched it lightly with the tips of his fingers, then turned away as the pain scored deep inside him.

There was a straight-backed chair in the corner of the room and he went and sat down, his silver eyes locked to the small, still figure lying in the bed. So much pain, so many regrets—yet at the beginning it had been so different.

He closed his eyes and opened his mind to the memories he had held at bay for so long, letting them fill each and every one of his senses, as Anna had filled them from the beginning. . .

It had started to rain so suddenly that day that it had caught everyone unawares. There had been much shouting and laughter as they had gathered up the picnic baskets from the riverbank and run back to the cars. Riccardo had been the last to leave, taking his time closing the huge wicker hamper.

He had noticed the girl not long after they had arrived and for the past hour had found himself watching her, drawn by her stillness, her total concentration as she bent over the small easel, by the tantalising glimpses he caught of her face beneath the brim of that huge, ridiculous straw hat with its cluster of brilliant-hued flowers.

The wind rose in a sudden little eddy and he heard her cry out as it whipped the sheet of paper out of her hands and carried it towards the water. He abandoned the basket, his long legs covering the distance in no time at all, and he caught the painting just as it was about to fall into the water. He turned it over, seeing the talent in the sure strokes of her brush which had captured the scene so clearly before the rain had started to make the paint run.

'Oh, thank you. . .*grazie.*'

She had a soft voice, faintly husky because she'd come running over the grass and was out of breath. She took the picture from him, murmuring in distress as she saw the streaks of paint running down it. 'Oh, what a shame!'

'Indeed, *signorina.* It showed exceptional talent.'

'Oh, do you think so? That's awfully kind.' She looked up, staring directly at him for the first time, and Riccardo felt as though he had been physically hit by the force of emotion he experienced staring into those huge deep green eyes.

He looked away, shocked by his own reaction, unable to understand the sudden urge which made him ache to take the girl into his arms and never let her go again, and he heard her give an embarrassed little laugh, obviously not understanding his silence.

'Well, I mustn't keep you any longer. Thank you for rescuing my painting, *signore. Grazie.*'

Riccardo watched her turn away, the brim of her hat shading her face, but he could recall with vivid clarity each of those delicate features, the pure deep green of her eyes, and knew in that moment that he couldn't let her go!

'Wait! How are you getting back to town?' He looked round as he asked the question, tall and faintly arrogant, seemingly oblivious to the rain which was beating down on them.

The girl hesitated, obviously unsure what to

answer. She looked up at the sky, then pulled the straw hat off her head with a wry little grimace. Her hair spilled over her shoulders and halfway down her back in silky red waves, and Riccardo felt his mouth go dry. His hands clenched at his sides; the desire to reach out and touch those shimmering red waves was so great that he almost groaned aloud as he held himself in check.

'Well, the same way I got here, I suppose.' She gave a soft little laugh. 'I walked because it was such a beautiful day, but I think I may live to regret it, don't you? Still, a drop of rain never killed anyone.'

She tucked the ridiculous hat into a large canvas bag, then piled the rest of her equipment together, glancing up at Riccardo as she finished with a smile which held a wealth of gentle amusement. 'You're going to get awfully wet standing there like that.'

No one ever teased him. No one ever had, even when he was a child. He'd been brought up to expect deference, to expect people to listen to what he said then agree with every word. No one in his world would have dared to make even a gentle joke at his expense. But this girl did.

She looked at him and smiled, because all she saw was a man acting rather foolishly by standing in the rain. She didn't see Riccardo Falcone and all that the name implied. She just saw him as a man like any other, and it was a heady experience to know that the amusement warming her green eyes was solely for him, that the awareness he also saw there was because she found *him* attractive.

'I shall drive you back to town. Come.'

'Oh, but that isn't necessary.' Suddenly her voice had a slight edge to it, the softness overlaid with a determination which made his elegant black brows rise, and he saw her face flush. She looked away, twisting the strap of her bag in her fingers, obviously embarrassed. 'I mean, I wouldn't dream of putting you to such trouble when your friends are waiting.'

Almost on cue Riccardo heard a voice calling him, but he didn't bother to look round and acknowledge it, even though he recognised it as belonging to Sofia. 'It is no trouble. As for my friends. . .' He gave a very Latin shrug, his thin lips curling into a smile of dismissal, yet for some reason that seemed to annoy the girl.

She swung the bag onto her shoulder, her green eyes sparkling as they met his. 'Maybe you don't care if they are inconvenienced, but I'm afraid I do. Thank you for your kind offer, *signore*, but I shall have to refuse. Goodbye.'

She headed up the bank towards the road, not bothering to look back as she turned in the direction of the town. Riccardo watched her go, anger awakening inside him. He wasn't used to being refused. People always did as he told them to, but seemingly his wishes had meant nothing to the girl.

'Riccardo, *caro*, come, we are waiting.' Sofia made her way carefully down the bank to him. Her fingers curled possessively around his arm as she glanced at the small figure walking determinedly along the road. 'There is a problem, *caro*? You know that girl?'

He could hear the jealousy in her voice and it

irritated him even more. Many women had sought to possess him, but all had been disappointed—as Sofia would be disappointed, if that was what she hoped for. He moved away so that Sofia's hand fell from his arm, his handsome face cold. 'I have no idea who she is. Go back to the car, Sofia, I shall bring the hamper.'

It took only minutes to load the basket into the boot of the red Ferarri. Riccardo started the engine, pushing the wet black hair out of his eyes as he waved to the others as they roared past. He glanced at Sofia, seeing the tightness of her mouth, and held back a sigh. He didn't want to have to deal with one of her tantrums today. He couldn't be bothered.

He leant across, turning her head to take her mouth fully beneath his while his tongue forced its way between her lips until he could feel her go soft and pliant in his arms.

'*Caro. . .caro. . .*'

She clung to him, murmuring soft little endearments as he let his mouth trail up to her temple, reassured by his passion. But his silver eyes were looking past her, focused on the girl in the distance. . .

The girl in the bed shifted restlessly. If she had dreamed in the past few days she didn't remember, yet suddenly her mind was full of voices and pictures from the past and she clung to them, needing them to fill the dark, empty spaces which scared her so much. . .

* * *

Nell still wasn't back by the time Anna finished dinner that night, but that didn't surprise her. They had agreed before they'd come on the trip that each would go her own way. She and Nell had been friends for years, even before they had both started at art college, and such an agreement put no strain on their friendship.

The air was warm when she left the small hotel, so that it was hard to believe that just a short while before there had been such a downpour—harder still to believe that that meeting down by the river had actually happened. Had she really met that man or had she dreamt him, drifting off in the heat of the sun to awake abruptly when it had started to rain?

Anna closed her eyes and immediately his face sprang to mind—those burning silver eyes watching her so intently, that thin-lipped mouth curling up at the corners, almost as though smiling was something he didn't do very often. . .

A shiver ran down her spine and she opened her eyes abruptly. He had been only too real, but she would never see him again and really she wasn't sorry. There had been something about him which disturbed her!

Anna took her time as she wandered through the town, stopping when she came to the café at the corner of the piazza. She sat down at one of the outside tables and ordered coffee. It came in a small white cup, thick and rich, and she sipped it slowly, enjoying the taste and fragrance which seemed so much a part of this area of Italy.

'So, *signorina*, you are unharmed by the soaking you received?'

She recognised his voice at once, and that shocked her almost as much as hearing it again did. Somewhere deep in her mind she must have stored every nuance of those rich tones, and now, as she turned and saw him sitting at a table in the corner, she felt a frisson run down her spine. Just for a moment she met those incredible silver eyes then turned away, her heart beating wildly although she couldn't understand what was causing such a reaction. She could feel the blood pulsing through her body, feel it in every cell, as though suddenly she had come to life.

'I may join you?'

His hand rested on the back of the chair, yet Anna had a feeling that it was only lip-service to politeness which made him ask permission. She nodded, wishing for some strange reason that she could refuse, yet she seemed powerless to find the right words. He sat down beside her, stretching his long legs beneath the small table, his hard thigh brushing hers before she drew away.

'*Scusi, signorina.*' He snapped his fingers and the waiter rushed to take his order, coming back almost immediately with a glass of red wine. The man took a drink, then set the glass down, toying with the stem.

Anna couldn't seem to take her eyes off his hands. He had such elegant hands—broad-palmed, with long strong fingers, the olive skin deeply tanned. There was a faint scattering of dark hair on his wrists beneath the cuffs of an immaculate white silk shirt, plain gold links gleaming against the stark fabric.

Anna felt as though her mouth was stuffed with cotton as she continued to stare at those hands toying with the glass while the silence grew until she knew that she had to break it. There was something dangerous about the silence, about these feelings which filled it instead of words.

'You and your friends got home safely, then?'

'*Si.* We are staying just outside the town; I have a house there. You should have permitted me to drive you back. It was foolish to get so wet when there was no need.'

She flashed him a small look of annoyance, recalling all too clearly the reason why she'd refused. 'I would only have been in the way.'

He shook his head with that same arrogance she'd noticed earlier. 'If I chose to offer you a lift then that is the end of the matter.'

'And to hell with what anyone else wanted?' She couldn't believe she'd said that. She stared at him with huge green eyes which reflected her shock, but surprisingly he laughed.

'*Si*—to hell with what everyone else wanted. Does that shock you, *signorina*. . . I am sorry, but I do not know your name.'

'Becket—Anna Becket. And no, I don't suppose it does shock me. I get the impression that you do what you please.'

He inclined his head gravely, but there was mockery in his silver eyes and in the slight curl of his mouth. 'Indeed. You are very perceptive, Anna. I may call you that, I hope? And you must call me Riccardo, as that is my name—Riccardo Falcone.'

'Of course.' She ran the name through her mind, testing it. It suited him so well, she thought. There was something decidedly predatory about him, like the sleek hunting bird his name brought instantly to mind.

She studied him from under her lashes, her artist's eyes seeing the perfection of the bone structure beneath the flesh. His features were finely drawn, from the elegant arch of his thick black brows to the straightness of his nose, with those slightly flaring nostrils. He was a handsome man, undoubtedly, but something told her that he could be ruthless when he chose, and a shiver ran down her spine again.

'You are cold, Anna Becket? Perhaps you caught a chill from the rain this afternoon. You really should have accepted my offer, *cara*.'

His deep voice played upon the last word and Anna's face coloured. She wasn't sure that she liked him taking liberties on such short acquaintance. It implied a degree of intimacy she wasn't ready for yet... She bit back a gasp, realising just how her mind was racing ahead. She had no idea who Riccardo Falcone was, yet here she was speculating that they would meet again!

She put down her cup and got up unsteadily, forcing a smile which didn't quite hide the anxiety in her green eyes. She had come to Tuscany to fulfil a lifelong dream, and getting involved with anyone—especially someone like this man, who disturbed her so—had no part in it. 'I really must go. My. . .my friend will be wondering where I am if I'm late back.'

He rose too, his silver eyes glittering with something she didn't understand. 'So, Anna, you are not here alone? You are with someone?'

His deep voice was flat now, the rich tones clipped, and in a sudden flash Anna realised that he was angry—but why? She looked at him in confusion. 'I. . . Yes, of course. Nell and I came on holiday together, but she went to Florence today to see some of the galleries while I stayed here to paint by the river.'

He gave a sudden laugh. 'Nell? I see. You are with a girlfriend, then?'

Anna nodded then flushed hotly as she suddenly understood what he had thought—although what business it was of his whom she was with, she had no idea. 'Yes! We arrived three days ago and intend to make the most of this trip. We've been saving for ages to come here.'

'Then you must permit me to show you both a little of the charm of Tuscany. Perhaps you and your friend would join me at my villa tomorrow for lunch. I promise you that you will not be disappointed. The scenery is magnificent.'

Anna shook her head, still annoyed by his temerity. She had the feeling that given half the chance Riccardo Falcone would try to take over her life, and she had no intention of allowing him to do that! 'I'm afraid it's out of the question—'

'Nonsense. I insist.' He cut her off, smiling in a

way which made the blood start to swirl through her veins despite her annoyance. 'I shall collect you both tomorrow at noon. It will be my way of apologising.'

'Apologising?' Anna could barely think straight. Did he know how potent that smile could be? Deep down she knew that he did, knew that Riccardo Falcone was well aware of its power and didn't hesitate to use it, but even that didn't lessen its effect.

He took her hand and raised it to his lips, his silver eyes holding hers in a look which made the heat flow through her veins. 'For allowing you to walk away from me this morning. . .and get wet.'

Anna drew her hand away, stunned by what she'd heard. He really was the most arrogant man she had ever met! Did he really imagine he could have stopped her simply by turning on the charm as he was turning it on now? Her green eyes glittered, but before she could say anything to set him straight he gave a husky laugh.

'Forgive me. I fear that I have offended you, and that was not my intention. I am afraid my English is not perfect.' He gave that very Latin shrug again, his wide shoulders straining the soft white silk, drawing her attention to his powerful physique—the flatly muscled torso, the narrow hips, those long, muscular legs.

Heat ran unchecked through Anna's whole body and she turned away, bumping into the table in her haste, wincing as the metal bruised her thigh.

'Careful, Anna.' He was beside her in an instant,

his long fingers closing around her arm as he steadied her, before with marked reluctance he let her go.

Anna took a long, slow breath, then forced herself to look up at him, 'I have to go.'

'*Si.* You do not wish to worry your friend. I understand, of course. But tomorrow, Anna, tomorrow you and I will have all the time in the world to talk.'

He gave her a slow smile, and something in the depths of his eyes made her heart leap painfully. Anna turned away, hurrying along the street as though a thousand demons were snapping at her heels, but when she reached the far end she couldn't stop herself looking back. . .

Riccardo Falcone was standing where she had left him, watching her. The sun had almost disappeared now, and the cypress trees in the centre of the square cast heavy shadows on the ground, but he was standing in the light spilling from the open door of the café. And it seemed to Anna, as everything else faded into the night, that they stood alone, she and Riccardo Falcone, locked into their own private world. . .

The pictures were starting to fade now, but she clung to them desperately, needing the past to open the door to the present, needing him even more. . .

'Ricco. . . Ricco!'

He felt the shock knife into him as he heard his name. Only one person had ever called him that—

only one had ever been allowed the privilege. Slowly, as though in a dream, his eyes opened.

Anna was sitting up in bed, her face still pale, but there were twin spots of colour in her cheeks, the glaze of fear in her huge green eyes. Yet even as he watched she focused on him.

She held her hands out, her mouth curling into the smile he recalled so well and had once never thought to see again.

'Oh, Ricco, darling. I was dreaming about you, then I suddenly woke up and. . .' She looked round in sudden confusion, her voice going hoarse with mounting fear. 'Where am I? What has happened? Ricco. . .!'

He got up from the chair and went to the bed to take her outstretched hands, so many emotions filling him that he felt suddenly as though he would explode. Just for a moment he stared into her face, his eyes searching, searching. . . Then slowly he drew her into his arms and held her as though he would never let her go again.

'You are in the hospital, *cara*.'

'Hospital!'

He felt her tense, felt the quiver which raced through her slender body as she tried to absorb what he had told her, and his heart missed a beat as he waited to see what other reaction the information would trigger.

She drew back abruptly, her face very pale, her eyes luminous with alarm. 'But why? How. . .?'

He took her back into his arms and held her close, his hand gentle at her nape. 'Shh, *cara mia*. Do not distress yourself. You are recovering from an accident, and that is all that is important.'

'But I can't remember... I can't remember how it happened or...or anything about it! Ricco, I'm scared!'

'There is no need. I am here, Anna. I shall always be here. You are quite safe. Everything will be all right now, *cara*...'

She nestled her head against him, as though suddenly drained by everything, a sigh leaving her slender body as she gave herself up to the strength and comfort his arms offered. 'I know. So long as you are here, then it will be all right, darling. I know that. Just hold me, please, then I know I am safe.'

He held her to him, his lips tender against her temple, his hands gentle as they cradled her, but anyone watching would have been shocked by the ferocity of his expression, the burning glitter of determination in his silver eyes.

He had been granted the impossible. But he would take the gift he'd been given, take it and use it, no matter that deep down he knew it was a gift he should have refused.

He, Riccardo Falcone, was going to do the impossible and turn back the clock...!

CHAPTER TWO

'ARE you tired, *cara*? Perhaps you should rest before we make the journey to the villa.'

Anna laughed softly, reaching over to brush Riccardo's lean cheek with a kiss. 'How can I be tired? I've done absolutely nothing! It really was dreadfully extravagant of you to hire that plane. We could have booked onto a scheduled flight.'

Riccardo shrugged, slipping the key into the ignition as he started the engine of the small, powerful car with a throaty roar. 'On a scheduled flight you would have had the inconvenience of other people. This was more restful for you.'

Anna laughed again, delighting in his thoughtfulness. He had spoiled her terribly, spending every minute of each day with her in the hospital before poor Dr Lewis had finally been bullied into letting her leave. The trouble with Riccardo was that he was so used to having his own way that it never crossed his mind that people wouldn't agree to his demands, and, because of that, they usually did!

'You can't wrap me in cotton wool for ever, and really there is no need, Ricco,' she admonished gently. 'I'm fine—absolutely fine. In fact I can't remember feeling this marvellous in ages.'

He shot her a swift glance, his silver eyes narrowed, a sudden tension about him that she couldn't really understand. 'What do you mean, Anna?' He must have seen her surprise at the sharpness in his voice because his face smoothed out. He reached for her hand, brushing her knuckles with his lips, laughing softly when he felt her shudder. 'You seem to have no problem with remembering how I make you feel, my darling. But you never mentioned that you had been feeling unwell before the accident? Why did you say nothing?'

Anna looked away, feeling suddenly tense. Dr Lewis had explained everything to her at the hospital—how she had lost her memory for a short time and that it wasn't unusual after the kind of head injury she'd suffered. He had dwelt on the positive side of her rapid recovery, yet sometimes she had the strangest feeling that there was still something missing—like just now, when off the top of her head she'd made that statement. She knew that it was true, but there was no depth to the knowledge—it was like a dream feeling which still lingered when one awoke, insubstantial yet haunting.

'Anna?'

She roused herself, not wanting to see that look of concern on Riccardo's face again, not wanting anything to cloud their happiness. 'I don't think it was a question of not telling you, darling. There was nothing to tell! It's just that this last week has been so wonderful, almost. . .well, almost like falling in love with you all over again.' She gave a soft little laugh. 'Not many couples are lucky enough to experience that, so maybe there was a hidden blessing to my accident—the old silver lining to the cloud, in fact!'

His face cleared and he smiled at her, such love in his eyes that Anna felt her throat lock on a spasm of intense joy. He bent over and kissed her lingeringly, drawing back with a wry smile as he felt her immediate response. 'Remember what the good doctor said, *cara mia*. Not too much excitement until you are completely recovered from your injuries.'

Colour tinted her cheeks and she looked away from Riccardo's knowing eyes, feeling the desire throbbing inside her like an ache which wouldn't go away. 'Dr Lewis is a killjoy!'

'*Si*, but he also has your welfare at heart, so we must obey his rules. . .for a while.'

There was an open promise in Riccardo's deep voice, and Anna smiled as she turned to look out of the window while he eased the car out of the parking space. She hadn't been exaggerating when she'd said that it was like falling in love with Riccardo all over again. There was a newness to each soft kiss they shared, an underlying passion heightened by the restrictions which Dr Lewis had laid down.

She frowned, catching sight of her reflection as they passed into some shadows, her hand lifting to touch the exquisite silk turban that Riccardo had brought her that morning to cover her poor hair.

Had the doctor simply meant that she mustn't rush her recovery from the operation, or what? He had seemed oddly ill at ease in the last day or so. Anna had gained the impression that there was something he'd wanted to speak to her about, but each time it had ended up unsaid. But what in all truth could there be to worry about? She had her memory back, her injuries were healing and, although it seemed impossible, she and Riccardo had never been closer than they had been these past few days.

She turned to glance at him, studying the strong lines of his classical profile. She loved him so much that she couldn't imagine what life would be like without him—didn't want to try. With Riccardo she was whole; without him she was nothing but an empty shell. . .

She shivered, wondering where the thought had come from, startled by the bitter pain it aroused. She searched her mind, but as sometimes happened, she'd discovered lately, the harder she tried to find an answer the more it eluded her. It had been such a silly thought anyway, because since she and Riccardo had met they had never been apart—although at the beginning Anna had been determined that she wasn't going to fall under his spell!

'What are you thinking about, my darling?' Ricco laughed, his gaze tender as he let it linger on her for a moment. 'There is such a sparkle to your eyes. . .'

Anna laughed with him, reaching across to touch his arm, feeling the warm, hard muscles beneath the smooth cloth of his light grey suit. 'You. . .as if you need to ask! My thoughts have been with you constantly for the past week, Riccardo.'

'*Bene*! A wife should think about her husband, *si*?' He teased her gently, his voice full of light amusement, and Anna relaxed back in the seat, enjoying the chance just to be with him this way. Riccardo had an undeniable charisma and it still drew her to him, kept him at the centre of her world.

'Mmm, that sounds smugly self-confident, Riccardo Falcone! What would you say if I told you that I had no intention of ever seeing you again after that night we met in the square, that I went back to the hotel and made up my mind that you were just about the most arrogant man I had ever met?'

He shrugged as he drew the car to a slow halt to join the flow of traffic heading away from the airport. 'What I would say is that it is a good job I managed to change your mind, because my life would have been empty without you, *cara*.'

'As mine would have been.' Anna gave a soft little laugh. 'If you hadn't guessed that I would go back to the river the next day then we might never have met again. Nell was incensed when I told her about your invitation to lunch at your villa and that I had no intention of going. She was longing to see inside it and tried her hardest to persuade me, but I wouldn't budge!

'I told her that I had no idea who you were—that you could be an axe murderer for all I knew! Why, she even went rushing off to speak to Signora Manetti who ran the hotel, to ask her if she knew anything about you just to set my mind at rest. . . What is it, Ricco?' Anna straightened, startled by the sudden expression which had crossed Riccardo's face.

He shook his head, easing the car into a gap in the traffic. 'Nothing, *cara*. I was just concentrating on the traffic, that is all. So what did the redoubtable Signora Manetti say? I must assume that it was nothing too dreadful—nothing to make you believe you need worry—because you've never mentioned this before?'

Anna shook her head, watching him from under her lashes, seeing the grey tinge beneath his tanned skin. Had something upset Riccardo—but what? 'No. But I don't think she could understand Nell's rotten Italian anyway, so she probably didn't have any idea what she was being asked.'

He shrugged indifferently. 'Perhaps. However, your fears did prove groundless, didn't they? And I, for one, am glad that I managed to guess where you would be. To have you for my wife has been my greatest joy, Anna.'

There was no doubting his sincerity, his rich voice was full of emotion. Anna smiled shakily, chasing away the brief moment of uncertainty as she let her head rest back against the seat. The past week must have been hard for Riccardo, so it was little wonder that he seemed tense at times. But there was nothing to worry about. Fate had been kind that day, by allowing Riccardo to find her.

Her eyes drifted shut as tiredness combined with the motion of the car lulled her into a sleep filled with so many happy memories. . .

* * *

They collected the makings of a picnic lunch on their way down to the river. Nell, always good-natured, had stopped grumbling about the missed opportunity to see inside a villa and had gone wandering off with her camera to capture the colours of the fields on the far side of the river to use in one of her tapestries.

Anna waved her off with a feeling of relief, then set up her easel. She loved Nell dearly, but not even to Nell could she explain the real reason for her reluctance to accept the invitation. When she had got back to the hotel the night before she had tried her hardest to put Riccardo Falcone out of her mind, but it had proved impossible. He had haunted her dreams all night long—dreams which made her blush even now to remember them!

Dragging the battered straw hat out of her bag, she put it on, but the heat in her cheeks owed less to the sun than it did to the thoughts filling her head, and she made a determined effort to chase them away. She wouldn't waste time thinking about him. . .she absolutely refused to do so!

She got out her paints, collected water from the river in a small glass jar, then determinedly set to work. She was soon engrossed in capturing the gentle beauty of the scene, so that when a shadow fell over the paper she didn't bother glancing up .

'It's coming along quite well, don't you think? Almost as good as yesterday but there's something missing. . .'

'A little more shade here. . .and here.'

A long, lean finger lightly touched the paper, then

withdrew out of her line of vision. Anna stayed quite still, feeling her heart pounding, the sudden clamminess of her palms.

'You do not agree, Anna?' He gave a soft laugh which made the hair on the back of her neck lift. 'Perhaps you consider me to be too presumptuous in making such an observation. I apologise. I shall try to make up for it over lunch.'

She got up slowly, waiting until she was on her feet before she looked at him, but it didn't help. There was still that strange tightness in her throat, the feeling that her heart was ricocheting around her chest. 'What are you doing here? Did. . .did you follow me?'

Riccardo shrugged, his hands pushed deep into the pockets of his beige trousers. The breeze had blown a lock of black hair across his brow, and it gave him a rakish air heightened by the mocking challenge that she saw in his silver eyes as they studied her.

Anna was instantly conscious of her appearance—the simple sleeveless green cotton dress with its long flowing skirt, the espadrilles laced on her bare feet. A strand of hair had worked free from the plait she'd woven it into that morning and it blew across her cheek now, catching the sunlight so that it seemed to burn like a flame.

Riccardo's eyes fell to it and he reached out, his fingers lingering against its softness before he brushed it behind her ear in the lightest of gestures, yet Anna felt the touch in every cell of her body. Her breath caught and her breasts pushed against the soft cotton, the nipples hard and taut as her body responded of its own volition and beyond her control.

Shocked and afraid, she turned away at once, stripping the painting from the easel, her hands shaking as she slid it into a folder and started gathering her paints together.

'No.' He stopped her with a light hand on her arm, his face suddenly set, his mouth thinning with displeasure. 'There is no need to run away. I did not follow you, Anna Becket. I merely deduced that I might find you here again today. However, it is obvious that you do not welcome my company so I shall leave. It was never my intention to spoil your day, nor my desire to frighten you. If I have done either, then I apologise.'

He turned to leave, the rigid set of his back an accusation in itself for her rudeness and stupidity. He hadn't scared her—at least not in the way he meant! It had been her own unexpected response to him which had done that, but that wasn't any excuse. She was a grown woman of twenty, and should be able to handle her response to a handsome man who was showing interest in her with an adult poise, yet she was acting like a silly teenager!

She dropped the paint box onto the springy grass and ran after him, catching his arm to make him stop. 'Wait! It is I who should apologise, Riccardo. I was incredibly rude and there was no reason to be. It's just that. . .just that. . .'

'That you do not know what I want with you and it makes you afraid.' He laughed deeply, the self-mockery she saw in his face startling her almost as much as his alarming perception.

She felt the heat run into her face and looked down so that the brim of her hat shaded it from that searching gaze, then found her eyes flying up again when he continued, his deep voice slow and oddly strained, as though he found the words hard to say.

'I, too, am afraid, Anna—because I, too, do not understand fully what is happening. Perhaps that makes us soul mates, *si*?'

'I. . .' She didn't know what to say. She could feel the colour ebbing and flowing in her face as she stared at him with confused green eyes. She couldn't imagine Riccardo Falcone being afraid of anything, yet there was no doubting the sincerity she'd heard, no denying the glitter of uncertainty that she could see in his silvery eyes.

'Have lunch with me, Anna, then maybe we can both find some answers.' He gave a soft laugh, his hand reaching out to tilt her chin just a fraction as he stared at her. 'And maybe they will be answers which make sense of something which makes so little right at this moment.'

She wanted to refuse; she could hear the polite little words echoing inside her head—words which would put an end to a situation which was running fast and furiously out of her control as each second passed. But the words she heard inside her weren't the words which came out. 'All right then, I will have lunch with you, Riccardo. But you must understand that is all I am agreeing to—just lunch and nothing else.'

'Of course.' He nodded gravely. 'Once lunch is over then I shall drive you back to your hotel and that will be the end of it.'

Would it? Anna turned away to collect her things, packing them haphazardly into her bag before she went in search of Nell. But in her heart she'd known even then that it wouldn't be the end—as he had known it. . .

'Anna, wake up, *cara*. We have arrived.'

Anna blinked, yawning delicately as the soft voice roused her. She opened her eyes and smiled when she found Riccardo bending over her, his handsome face so close that she could simply reach up and press her mouth to his. He kissed her back, his lips hardening with passion for a moment, before he made himself draw back with a wry grimace.

'You should not tempt me like that, my love. You know how hard I find it to resist—especially when we have been apart for so long.'

Anna frowned. 'So long? What do you mean, Ricco?'

Something crossed his face before he turned away to withdraw the key from the ignition. When he looked back at her there was a half-smile on his mouth, an awareness in his eyes as they travelled over her face. 'That time you spent in hospital, *cara*, seemed like an eternity to me.'

She gave a soft little laugh, savouring the headiness of her power over him. With everyone else Riccardo was so cool and aloof that she knew most people were in awe of him, but he had never been like that with her. 'A year of marriage and you still feel that way. . . What a compliment, my love!'

It was such gentle teasing that she felt shocked to see the way he stiffened all of a sudden. His hand clenched around the keys and Anna gasped as she saw a trickle of blood run between his fingers. 'Ricco, darling, look what you've done! What's wrong?'

He glanced down, almost as though he hadn't felt the pain before, then seemed to make an obvious effort to collect himself. 'It is nothing. Do not concern yourself, Anna.'

He made to get out of the car but she stopped him, unable to explain why she felt so scared. She thought back over what she'd said, but nothing seemed to explain his reaction to that light remark—unless. . .

'Were you thinking about the accident? About how lucky we are that we will have more years together? I still can't believe myself just how kind fate has been.' She shuddered. 'I have nightmares sometimes, thinking about how I might never have recovered my memory. Although I can't believe that I would have forgotten you!'

'You are right, of course, Anna. I too have nightmares, but we must put it all behind us. All that is past and now we have the future to look forward to—our future together.'

He kissed her hard and hungrily, then let her go and got out of the car. Anna waited for him to come round and open her door, smiling as he helped her out. This was where she had fallen in love with

Riccardo; they had been so happy then, so much happier than they had been recently. . .

She caught her breath, watching blankly as Riccardo lifted the cases from the boot and carried them towards the house. She wanted to shut out that fleeting thought, but now that it had been set free it was impossible. At some point in the past she and Riccardo hadn't been happy—but why? The question troubled her because she couldn't recall the answer to it.

'We had lunch outside in the garden that first day you came here, Anna. Do you remember?'

Anna forced a smile, hoping that Riccardo wouldn't notice how strained it was. She didn't want to start worrying him, but the thought that they had once been deeply unhappy had troubled her throughout the meal. She glanced up as the housekeeper came and cleared the dessert plates, but the woman barely acknowledged her before she carried the dishes indoors.

Anna sighed. 'I remember, Ricco. It was a marvellous day, just like today, but Carla was here then, serving the lunch, and she was so friendly—not at all like Maria.'

Riccardo picked up his glass of wine. 'I understand how you feel, my darling, but Carla and Guido have had to travel to Pisa as I told you.' He shrugged lightly, but the hand holding the glass tightened. 'Some family business, I believe. I was lucky to get Maria at such short notice, as soon it will be the height of the season and many people will be requiring the services of such an excellent cook.'

Anna felt suitably rebuked and looked down, toying with her own glass of sparkling mineral water. She was probably tired, despite the sleep she'd had on the way here, and allowing small things to bother her which wouldn't have done so normally.

'What is it, *cara*? Tell me. There is no need to keep anything locked inside you when I might be able to help.'

Riccardo touched her hand, concern in his deep voice, and Anna told herself to stop being such a baby. It wasn't fair to keep worrying him like this. She turned her hand over, capturing his long fingers in her smaller ones, studying the contrast between their skin tones for a moment before she smiled up at him. 'I'm sorry. I was just a bit disappointed that Carla wasn't here. I suppose I wanted everything to be just as it was that first time. . .perfect!'

She gave a light laugh, trying to brush aside the odd feelings she'd had since she walked into the house. Everything was just as it had always been—the elegant old furniture, the exquisite paintings, the rich tapestries Nell had drooled over that first day. It was just she who was different, and it was no wonder really. Losing her memory must have been a huge trauma, and she obviously still hadn't fully recovered from the after-effects.

'Of course.' Riccardo lifted her hand to his lips and kissed the soft palm, smiling at her as he did so, yet Anna could still see the shadows in his eyes.

They haunted her, made her feel guilty knowing that she was the cause of them.

'There is no "of course" about it! I'm just a spoilt brat—although you have only yourself to blame for that, Riccardo Falcone!'

His mouth curled, his silver eyes brilliant now as they held hers in a look which made Anna feel all sorts of things—and nothing Dr Lewis would approve of! 'Indeed? So I am to blame for you being—what was the word?—a brat? Is this some very British piece of logic which escapes my poor Italian mind?'

'I doubt anything escapes you, Ricco! You are far too astute. But, yes, you are to blame for turning me into a petulant woman by spoiling me so much in the past week.' She gave a mock sigh. 'I suppose it can't last, so I'll just have to get used to it. Once we're back in Milan everything will revert to normal!'

'And is normal so bad, *cara*?'

Was she imagining it, or was there an edge to the melodious tones now? Anna couldn't decide, but it bothered her. Was there a reason why Riccardo should believe she wasn't happy with their life in the big gracious house in Milan? She searched her mind, trying to recall what had happened when they had been there last.

It must be only a matter of a few weeks, because the accident had happened shortly after they'd arrived in London—although Anna still couldn't remember a thing about it. Yet try as she might she could barely recall what the house looked like, let alone anything else.

'No, of course not. I. . . I was just teasing, *caro*.' She pressed her fingers to her temple, feeling the pain throbbing against her skull. She'd had these sudden violent headaches each time she had tried too hard to force herself to concentrate. Dr Lewis had explained that they were nothing to worry about, simply a defence mechanism—although Anna couldn't really understand what he'd meant. Why should she need any kind of defence against her own memories?

'Your head is hurting, Anna? Why don't you lie down for a while? Travelling has been more tiring than you realise, and it would be foolish to hinder your recovery when you have now made such excellent progress.'

Anna forced a smile, relieved to agree with such a simple explanation. The journey had taken its toll, so it was little wonder that she was starting to imagine things. 'Yes, you're right. I am tired. If you don't mind, I think I will lie down for a while.'

Riccardo got up as she rose from the table, his hand sliding around her waist as he drew her close for a moment and brushed a light kiss over the top of her head. 'Would you like me to come upstairs with you, darling?'

She shook her head. 'No, I'll be fine. You stay out here and enjoy the afternoon sunshine. It will make a pleasant change after England's grey skies!'

She could feel him watching her as she walked back inside the house. She turned to look back and smiled, feeling the warmth running through her as she saw the expression of concern on his handsome face. Riccardo loved her, and it showed in everything he did and said.

She carried on up the stairs to the huge airy room they shared and slipped off her shoes before lying down on the bed with its antique white cotton coverlet, the smile still curving her mouth, the warmth still flowing through her body.

She was a very lucky woman to have a husband like Riccardo, although for some reason Nell, of all people, had been so against them marrying. What was it that Nell had said once. . .that Riccardo was a man with a past?

A cold chill ran through her, stealing the warmth and languor from her limbs. When the bedroom door opened she started nervously, watching as Riccardo came across the room. He stopped by the bed, staring down at her, and for a moment Anna felt her heart thunder wildly, as though she had been caught doing something she shouldn't.

'What is it now, Anna? Something is still troubling you, I can tell.' He sat beside her, taking her hand so that he immediately felt her slight start of shock—but then why should she be shocked? Riccardo had always possessed an almost startling perception, and she had never attempted to hide her feelings from him before. It bothered her that she should consider doing so now, and that in itself spurred her into telling him.

'I was thinking about something Nell said before we married.'

He grimaced. 'You must not live too much in the past, my love. It is the future which is all-important—our future together.'

The chill started to lift, and she smiled at him more naturally this time. 'I know, but I keep getting these odd flashes...' She sighed. 'I expect they will stop when my memory comes back completely; I hope that they will.'

'I am sure that is what will happen. But if something is troubling you then tell me, Anna. Do not worry about it alone when you can share it with me.'

She lifted his hand to her cheek and held it there. 'Like we have always shared things, Ricco. I think that is what makes our marriage so special. But this is nothing earth-shattering—just some silly remark Nell once made about your being a man with a past, whatever that may mean!'

He laughed, but there seemed to be a note of strain in it.

'I have never made any attempt to lie to you about the fact that there were women in my life before we met, Anna, if that is what you mean.'

Anna laughed too, wondering if it was embarrassment which had put that edge in Ricco's voice. But embarrassment and Riccardo seemed like a contradiction in terms! 'Mmm, I never imagined that you had led the life of a monk, Ricco!'

He smiled at her teasing, bending down to brush her mouth with his before he stood up. 'And I have never claimed to have been one. But you are the only woman in my life now, Anna—the only woman

I shall ever want. Now, try to get some rest. I only came to see if there was anything you needed.'

'Nothing, thank you, darling. I have everything I need.' She knew he understood what she meant as his eyes blazed back at her. He brushed her cheek with his fingers in the lightest caress, then turned and left the room, closing the door quietly beind him as he went.

Anna stared up at the ornate ceiling, feeling the warm glow of happiness inside her. Losing her memory had been a dreadful experience made sweeter by the joy of rediscovering how much Riccardo loved her. But then, she had never doubted that. . .

She stared at the plaster vines and bunches of grapes on the ceiling without seeing them as the realisation hit her that it wasn't the thought of the women he had once known which was nagging at the back of her mind but something else, something in Riccardo's past—but what?

Suddenly she knew that if she discovered the answer to that then she would find the key to so much more. And yet the thought filled her with a sudden fear of what that might be.

CHAPTER THREE

ANNA felt hot and sticky when she awoke some hours later. The light wool skirt and crêpe blouse which had been so suitable for the early English summer were far too hot for Tuscany. She swung her legs off the bed and walked to the window, throwing back the shutters to let in what little breeze there was.

The sun was low in the sky, settling a golden cast over the rolling hills. The Villa Margherita was some miles outside the town and there were no other buildings to restrict the view of the glorious countryside. For a few minutes Anna simply stood and drank in the sight, but surprisingly it did little to soothe the unease she'd awoken with. The thought of what might have happened in Riccardo's past had lingered and was still with her now—a disturbing echo which couldn't be quietened no matter how she tried.

She turned away from the view, suddenly impatient with herself. There was a simple way to settle it. She would ask Riccardo if anything had happened just before the accident to put such a thought into her head. That was the most likely explanation, but for now she was doing more harm than good by worrying herself this way.

Determined to be sensible, Anna stripped off her

clothes and wrapped herself in the silk robe she found unerringly in the huge oak cupboard. She seemed to have no difficulty in remembering where everything was, and that in itself was a small reassurance. If she could recall such trivial things as where she kept her robe then surely she couldn't have fogotten anything more vital? It was just her own uncertainty, a quite understandable self-doubt, which was casting a shadow over this very welcome holiday at the villa. Riccardo had been so wrapped up in his work lately that they'd hardly had any time together. . .

Anna walked through to the en suite bathroom, refusing to let herself try to remember anything more. It was the present which was important, not the past—the fact that she and Riccardo were together and even more in love than ever in this special place.

She was just switching on the shower when the faint sound of the telephone ringing caught her attention before the water gushed, blotting out the sound. But hearing the phone ringing now and thinking about Nell earlier reminded her sharply that it had been ages since she'd spoken to her friend. Did Nell know about the accident?

She frowned as she lathered her arm. Riccardo had not mentioned that Nell had called, so it seemed more than likely that her friend had no idea what had happened. Her name would be mud if she didn't ring Nell soon and bring her up to date; this evening would be best, before it slipped her mind again.

With that decided, she wrapped herself in one of

the huge fluffy towels hanging on the rail and went back to the bedroom, stopping when she saw Riccardo standing by the window. He had his back to her and didn't appear to have heard her, so for a moment Anna enjoyed the rare chance to study him without his being aware of it.

He had shed his suit jacket and rolled up the sleeves of his pale blue shirt to leave his tanned forearms bare. His shoulders were slightly hunched, but even that didn't detract from the elegant power of his lean body. Anna let her eyes roam down his back, following the tapering lines of his torso, the taut curve of his buttocks, the powerful length of his thighs, and felt her heartbeat quicken. To her artist's eyes his body was almost perfect in its shape and symmetry; to the eyes of the woman who loved him the "almost" was unnecessary!

Her loving gaze travelled back up, lingering on the back of his well-shaped head, and she frowned slightly. His hair had grown longer than he usually wore it, brushing the back of his collar and starting to curl slightly, yet she didn't recall noticing it before. Still, it suited him, and her fingers itched to touch its sleek blackness, to feel the silky coolness beneath her palms as she had done so often in the past when they had made love. . .

'Ricco.' She didn't even realise she had whispered his name until she saw him start. He swung round so fast that she took a step back, shocked by the expression she surprised on his face, by the tension she suddenly saw in his powerful body, by. . .by feelings she couldn't begin to make sense of! This was Riccardo, the man she loved, yet just for a moment looking at him then was like looking into the face of a stranger, and it scared her!

'Anna, I did not hear you. You startled me, *cara mia.*' He gave a low laugh, his face smoothing out, the coldness in his silver eyes melting as he came over to her, and she felt her blood start to flow again as she saw the stranger disappear and Riccardo standing before her once more. 'There is something wrong, my darling?'

She took a shaky little breath, forcing a light note to her voice, still shaken by what had happened yet not wanting him to know how much. 'No. I think we startled each other! What were you thinking about just now? You looked so. . .so strange.'

He shrugged, sliding his hands up her arms to come to rest on her bare shoulders. 'Nothing important, just some minor business problem. But nothing to concern you, my darling. . .nothing we need waste time discussing.'

His mouth was gentle as it skimmed over her shoulder and up the side of her neck, but it left behind a devastating trail.

Anna shuddered, feeling the exquisite sensations rippling through her in waves. She closed her eyes and let her head fall back as Riccardo's mouth moved to the pulse which was beating so wildly at the base of her neck. She could feel the gentle pressure of his lips against her skin, their sudden parting as his tongue touched the aching little spot, and the blood started to thunder through her veins until she felt dizzy with it.

'Ricco, darling. . .' Her voice was little more than a husky whisper but it held an invitation as old as time. She felt his hands tighten on her arms for a moment, almost as though he was undecided what to do, before he drew her to him and pressed her against him, letting her feel the arousal of his body. He kept her there for a moment that was all too brief, before slowly he put her from him.

'We must be sensible, Anna. We must remember what the good doctor advised, no matter how difficult it is.'

His voice held a note of wry amusement, but his silver eyes burned with an echo of the passion they both felt, and suddenly the last thing Anna felt like being right then was sensible!

She moved towards him, her green eyes heavy-lidded, her breasts pushing against the soft folds of the towel in a way that she knew Riccardo noticed. Sliding her arms around his neck, she ran her fingers through his hair, enjoying the reality of its cool silkiness as she had savoured the thought just minutes before.

'But what if I don't wish to be sensible, darling? What if the very last thing on my mind right now is Dr Lewis and his advice?' She gave a husky little laugh, letting her body brush against his, watching the thin line of colour which ran across his cheekbones, the tiny nerve which started to beat so wildly in his jaw.

'Anna, I know how you feel. Do you think I do not feel it as well?' His deep voice grated, the restraint he was imposing upon himself etching lines of strain on his face, and Anna felt her heart swell with love. He wanted her as much as she wanted him, but he would do nothing which he thought might hurt her. How stunned his friends and colleagues would be, because he was known as a man who took what he wanted without thought for others—but then Riccardo had always been so different with her. And sometimes even Riccardo Falcone needed showing the way!

'Well if that is how you feel Ricco...' She gave a light shrug feeling the towel slipping away from her and making absolutely no attempt to stop it from falling. It landed on the floor at her feet, and in the silence the soft sound of it pooling on the polished wooden boards seemed louder than a drumroll.

Anna stood where she was, unashamed of her nakedness in front of the man who was her husband. Riccardo must have seen her like this hundreds of times, so it wasn't embarrassment which kept her standing so still—not when she had planned on it happening. It was the expression on his face, that aching, bitter sadness which tore at her heart and made her cry out his name in sudden fear. 'Riccardo!'

His eyes lifted to hers, burning with emotion, yet Anna couldn't understand half of what she saw there. 'I love you Anna. As God is my witness, everything I have done and everything I must do in the future owes itself to that!'

'Ricco...!'

His mouth swallowed her hoarse cry, his lips hard and demanding holding no trace now of the gentleness he'd shown her before as his passion was unleashed, but hers rose at once to meet it. Anna welcomed the hot surge of desire, greeted it with a desperation stemming from fear. She had no idea what Riccardo had meant just now, but surely it didn't matter when they had this.

He murmured to her in Italian, soft words of love and encouragement, as he eased her down onto the cool cotton coverlet and ran his hands down her body. Anna could hear the rise and fall of his voice, and even though she couldn't understand all the words she knew what he was saying. There was no need for translations when their bodies spoke the same language. Each soft caress told her that he loved touching her, each kiss how much he wanted her, each shuddering breath how great his desire for her was growing.

When he stripped off his clothes, tossed them onto the floor then lay down beside her, she opened her arms and drew him to her, letting her body make the final declaration. And she heard with her heart his making the same commitment. She loved him and he loved her...that was all that really mattered.

'You look beautiful tonight, *cara*. The rest did you good.'

Anna smiled, her green eyes alight with teasing laughter. 'Mmm, but perhaps it wasn't just the rest?'

Riccardo joined in, but was it her imagination or was there just a hint of strain in his deep voice? Anna picked up her spoon and popped a tiny morsel of the iced pudding into her mouth while she studied him from under her lashes, but there was nothing on his face to worry her and she relaxed again.

'I do not think Dr Lewis would be too pleased with us tonight, *cara.* We must not allow our emotions to run away with us too often, no?'

His accent was more pronounced than usual, but then she had noticed many times that he always sounded far more Italian after they had made love. Perhaps it was simply the fact that instinctively he resorted to his native language when he held her and whispered to her, so that it ran over into the hours which followed. Whatever, it warmed her now to hear it and recall the delicious hour they had spent in each other's arms—time which, despite the doctor's well-meant advice, had done far more to speed her recovery than any amount of pills and potions!

'If you say so, Riccardo.' She laughed up at him, openly teasing. 'Perhaps it would be better if we slept in separate rooms, and that way neither of us would be tempted?'

She expected him to laugh, to reach across and kiss her in a loving punishment for her temerity; what she did not expect was to see the anger which suddenly crossed his face as he pushed his chair back from the table and got up.

'If that is what you wish, Anna, then of course.'

'Ricco!' She shot to her feet, alarm darkening her green eyes. 'I was joking, darling. Surely you knew that? What on earth is the matter?'

He seemed to make an effort to control himself,

but there was no denying the tension in him as he crossed the room and poured brandy into a balloon glass. He raised it to his lips, and Anna was shocked to see that his hand was shaking. She went to him, stopping a few feet away, her face very pale, the soft down of hair which covered her head in tiny ringlets catching the light.

'What is it? What did I say?' She took a swift breath, feeling the first stirrings of fear, a culmination of all the uncertainties which kept plaguing her. 'Did... did something happen before the accident? Something I don't remember? Did we argue and... and sleep apart in separate rooms?'

He tipped the glass back and swallowed the rest of the liquor, his face holding a brooding darkness. 'What makes you ask that?'

She shook her head, suddenly annoyed that she couldn't remember and that Riccardo seemed to be hedging. 'I don't know! It was only an idea. It makes sense of something which was bothering me before. I... I had a feeling that something happened in Milan just before we went away, but I can't remember what it was. It's so frustrating! There are gaps in my memory. I didn't realise it until recently, but they're there all the same!

'Oh, I can remember all the important things—like who I am, who you are, and even silly things like what Nell said—but I keep getting this feeling that there are bits missing, almost as though some of the pieces haven't been fitted into the puzzle. I can see what the whole picture is supposed to be, but not the details. That's why I need to keep asking you, Ricco. For now *you* are my memory!'

She willed him to understand, somewhat surprised that he didn't appear to. Surely Riccardo could imagine what it must be like for her to have to rely on him this way? Yet it seemed almost as though he didn't want to discuss the past at times.

'I understand how upsetting it must be for you, Anna.' He set the glass down, then reached for her hand, smoothing the delicate skin with his thumb. 'But we should be thankful that it is only such insignificant details you cannot remember, *cara*. The thought that you might have forgotten about me and our life together. . .' He shrugged, but his gaze was intent, searching.

Anna forced a smile, wondering why it made her feel uncomfortable to stand there and have him watch her, almost as though he was looking for answers—but maybe that was what he was doing. Riccardo probably felt strange himself about these gaps in her memory—might even feel hurt that she couldn't remember everything about their life together. And with his stiff pride he would find it impossible to make such an admission!

She smiled teasingly. 'I don't think I could ever forget *you*, Ricco! I love you too much for that. It's just odd things, as I said, and I don't suppose they really matter. It's just that it's irritating to keep wondering what went on. If there are any skeletons lurking in the cupboards then I would much prefer to know about them!'

He laughed huskily, bending to kiss her mouth

with gentle tenderness. 'Well, I, for one, know nothing about any skeletons, my darling. But you must not concern yourself too much about these small lapses. What matters most is that I have you here with me, safe. Everything else is of little consequence.'

He drew her into his arms, his chin resting on the top of her head. Anna slid her arms around his lean waist, loving the feel of his body pressed against hers. Riccardo was right, of course; the most important thing was that she had come through the ordeal. Yet she couldn't stop thinking about the teasing comment which had started this, and the fact that he hadn't really answered her questions.

He obviously sensed that something was still bothering her, because he tilted her face up so that he could look into her eyes. 'So, what is worrying you now, *cara*?' He brushed her forehead with a light kiss, a smile softening his mouth. 'What thoughts are racing through that pretty head?'

She hesitated, and heard him laugh. 'Come, Anna, tell me. Is it so difficult to share your thoughts with your husband?'

'No, of course not. It's just. . .just that I don't want to upset you again.'

His hold on her tightened before he relaxed and smoothed the flat of his hand down her spine, sending a shudder of response through her. She felt him smile against her temple, heard the echo of masculine amusement in his deep voice at the fact that his lightest touch should have such an instant effect on her—but then, it always had.

Riccardo had taken her in his arms that first day she had come to the villa, and even then, in her innocence, she had burned with desire for him—and it seemed that the flames had been alight ever since.

'You are still thinking about this long-forgotten quarrel we had, *si*?'

She drew back with a frown. 'So we did quarrel? I sensed there was something. . . And it was serious enough to make us decide to sleep in separate rooms? But what was it about?'

He sighed heavily. 'I find it hard to recall exactly what started it now. It seems so unimportant.' He shrugged, but his mouth was a tight line, and Anna wondered if she was being silly to rake up old incidents which might be better left forgotten. Yet the desire to know the truth was too strong to let it go.

'So when did it happen?'

He seemed to hesitate, as though weighing up his reply, and his deep voice was edged when he finally answered. 'The night before you. . .we left for England. It blew up out of all proportion and ended with you telling me that you would not sleep in our room that night. It was the first night we had spent apart in our married life and we had no chance to resolve the quarrel before you had your accident.'

She understood then what had been worrying him, and loved him all the more. He hadn't wanted her to remember that silly argument because he had been afraid that it would affect their happiness now!

She gave a soft little laugh, pressing a kiss to his throat. 'Well, I make you a solemn promise that it won't happen again! That's the first, last and only time that we are sleeping apart, Riccardo—no matter what we quarrel about in future!'

'Let us hope that we do not have any quarrels—especially not here in our special place. We always were so happy here, my love. Remember?'

'Oh, yes. There always was a special magic about this place—even the first time I came here. Which reminds me—did you let Nell know about my accident? Because if you didn't get a chance I shall ring her tonight.'

Riccardo let her go, walking over to the French doors which led out onto the terrace. They had been opened earlier, to let in the cool night air, but now he drew them to before glancing back at her.

'I'm afraid that won't be possible, Anna. There has been some trouble with the telephone lines—storm damage which has not been repaired yet.' He shot the bolt, missing her startled gasp. 'They have promised to do it soon, but who knows how long it will take? Unfortunately it means that you will have to leave your call until another time. Now, if you will excuse me for a moment, I need to have a word with Maria about the work her son will be doing in the gardens. With Guido away we do not want to let everything get too overgrown.'

He left the room and Anna made no attempt to stop him. She walked over to the windows he had just closed and stared out, but the night was dark and she could see nothing but her own reflection staring back at her. Why hadn't she mentioned the fact that she'd heard the telephone ringing earlier?

Why hadn't she simply asked Riccardo how she could have heard it if the lines were down? There had to be an explanation, so why had those questions been so impossible to ask?

The face in the glass stared back at her—ghostly, unreal. It was just a shadow, not her, an image with the same features but no emotions. Yet suddenly it seemed to Anna that the reflection *was* her. Until she could fill in all the gaps in her memory then she had no more substance than it had—no more depth. She had to find out what was missing and fit the last pieces into the puzzle, no matter that the idea of what she might discover suddenly terrified her.

Riccardo was still sleeping when Anna awoke just after six. She hadn't slept well, her mind too busy with all the uncertainties. Slipping from the bed, she made her way quietly into the bathroom then hurriedly dressed in white jeans and a soft, loose pink top, taking care not to wake him.

She paused for a moment, staring down at him as he slept, feeling the painful tugging of her emotions. He looked strangely vulnerable lying there, his handsome face unguarded, those piercing silver eyes closed. How could she think even for a moment that he would lie to her when there seemed no reason for it?

She felt as though she was betraying him by going in search of answers, but surely he would understand. He loved her as the woman he had married, but she wouldn't be that person again until she knew everything that had happened in her past.

The big square hall was empty, pale morning sunlight spilling through the windows, bringing to life the swirling pattern on the soft old rug. Anna hurried across it, her bare feet making little sound as she stepped onto the polished boards. The study door creaked as she opened it, but the noise wasn't loud enough to carry upstairs.

After closing the door behind her, Anna ran to the desk and stood staring at the telephone with her heart beating painfully fast. If she discovered that it was working and that Riccardo had been lying to her then what would she do? It was like opening Pandora's box and letting loose all kinds of evils, because she didn't know how she would cope with the knowledge that he had lied to her.

Anna closed her eyes while the uncertainty grew as the seconds ticked past, but what choice did she really have? Her palm was sticky with perspiration as she lifted the receiver, her heart pounding so hard that at first she could hear nothing except its beating. She took a long, slow breath then listened. Silence, glorious, total silence came from the telephone!

'Anna, what are you doing?'

She hadn't heard the door opening, nor the sound of his quiet footsteps crossing the room. Now the shock of hearing his voice made her cry out. She dropped the receiver, staring at it with huge guilty eyes as it swung back and forth on the end of the line.

Riccardo said something softly—perhaps a curse, perhaps a murmur of concern, she had no idea which—as he hurried to her and caught her by the shoulders. 'Are you all right? Say something, Anna.'

His fingers bit into her flesh, the sudden pain rousing her from her trance, and she took a quick little breath. 'Yes, I'm fine. I just didn't hear you come in.'

'Obviously.' He glanced at the telephone, his silver eyes narrowing as he bent to replace it on its rest, and Anna rushed to explain, driven by the guilt she felt for ever having doubted him.

'I just thought I would check to see if the line had been repaired, but it hasn't.'

He shrugged, as though it was of little importance. 'Perhaps later today, or tomorrow.' He ran a hand through his hair, then smiled at her, but his gaze was searching. 'I had not realised you were so anxious to get in touch with your friend. If it is that important then you must write to her. It will take only a day or two for the letter to reach her.'

She forced a smile, unable to explain why it made her feel uneasy to see Riccardo watching her so closely. 'It isn't that important. I just wanted to let Nell know what had happened, because heaven help me if she finds out later and I've not been in touch! You know what a mother hen she can be.'

'*Si*? But you must not worry yourself about it, Anna. Write your letter and I shall post it for you when I drive into Pisa later.'

'Pisa? You never mentioned that you were going there, Ricco.' She frowned and heard him give a soft laugh as he caught her hands and drew her to him. He had slipped a robe on to come downstairs, but beneath it he was naked. Anna could feel the heat of his body seeping into her flesh.

'I am not going out of choice, *cara*.' He drew her even closer, so that her soft curves fitted perfectly against his hard contours. 'Out of choice I would remain here with you all day, but there is a business matter I need to attend to and unfortunately it cannot wait.'

Anna nestled against him, loving to feel him holding her so close. What a fool she had been to doubt him! Riccardo loved her. He wouldn't lie to her. 'It will be so lonely here without you, darling. Can't you put your meeting off, please. . .?'

Her hand slipped inside the folds of his robe, and she felt the shiver which danced over his skin as her fingers brushed against him. He caught her hand, pressing it to his chest so that she could feel his heart beating heavily against her palm, and the shiver slid through her this time.

'You are a witch, Anna. You make me want to forget all about business, all about everything except you. . .' His mouth was hungry as it took hers, his desire very much in evidence as he pressed her even closer and let her feel what holding her was doing to him.

Anna gave herself up to the kiss, letting it fill her mind and her body and erase the last of those silly doubts. If there were questions which needed answering then they would be answered in time; her mind would slowly unlock the last secrets but they would be nothing dreadful, nothing to worry about.

So long as she had Riccardo, then what could she possibly need to worry about after all?

She returned his kiss eagerly, unable to hide her feelings—as she'd always been unable to do with Riccardo, right from the beginning—and she heard him sigh regretfully as he gently eased her away from him. He pressed another, far too quick kiss to her parted lips, his silver eyes betraying his need even as he moved away.

'I am afraid that it is a meeting which I cannot cancel. However, it should not take too long to conclude.'

Anna stifled her disappointment. 'Then of course you must go. In fact, why don't I come with you? If it won't take long then maybe we could have lunch later?'

He shook his head. 'I do not think that is wise. The trip would tire you unnecessarily, Anna, and you would be on your own while I was at my meeting. No, it is far better that you stay here and rest, and I promise that I shall come back just as quickly as I can.'

He left the study, giving Anna no chance to try and cajole him into letting her go. She glanced at the telephone, then turned and almost ran from the room.

With Riccardo beside her she had no difficulty in quietening all these silly little fears. Riccardo had a way of smoothing everything over, of making sense out of things which seemingly made little, but with him gone the day suddenly stretched before her, a gaping void to be filled only by uncertainty.

CHAPTER FOUR

It got hotter and hotter as the day wore on. Anna finally resorted to taking one of the old rattan chairs down to the very bottom of the garden, where a grove of olive trees made a welcoming patch of shade.

She let her head rest back against the cushions, but for some reason it was impossible to relax. Riccardo had left shortly after breakfast, kissing her and promising to return just as fast as he could. He had appeared just as attentive as ever, but there had been a curious distance about him which had told her that his mind had been elsewhere. He rarely discussed his business dealings with her, yet suddenly Anna wished that she had asked him more about this meeting he'd needed to attend.

She closed her eyes, trying to think of what she knew about his work, surprised to realise that it was very little. She knew that he owned an import and export business, which worked out of Milan and had offshoots in several other large Italian cities. That he made a vast profit from it was indisputable, because their lifestyle reflected it: the huge house in Milan, the summer retreat here in Tuscany, the frequent holidays. . .

Riccardo Falcone was a very rich man, and held

in great awe by his associates, but apart from that, Anna realised with shock, she knew nothing more.

She got up, strangely uncomfortable with the thought, although it had never bothered her before. She followed the path through the trees, too restless to sit still any longer. If Riccardo hadn't told her much about his business then it was simply because it had seemed unnecessary. The hours they spent together were all-consuming, so that there was no need for anything else, yet she couldn't shake off the feeling that it was strange she should know so little.

She stopped when she came to the far side of the grove. The ground sloped steeply away from here and she had a clear view of the town. It was further than it appeared, because up here the air was so clear that it lessened the distance. Anna stood drinking in the view, wishing suddenly that she had her paints with her.

Several of her works had been shown to some enthusiasm by one of the smart galleries in Milan in the last year, and she was fast gaining a reputation for her delicate watercolours which gave her a deep satisfaction. She loved being Riccardo's wife, but it was nice to have her own identity as well. It would also be a lot more beneficial concentrating on work than allowing her imagination to run riot, as it seemed to be doing lately!

Inspired by the thought, she turned back to collect what she needed, then stopped abruptly when she saw the man coming through the trees. He must have caught sight of her at almost the same moment because he came to an abrupt halt, looking unsure and ill at ease.

'*Scusi, signora.* I did not know that you were here.' He gave her a small bow, then made as though to leave, but Anna stopped him, suddenly curious as to his identity.

'Who are you?' She spoke in English, because he obviously understood, and he stopped at once, his face flushing, his hands nervously turning the long-handled secateurs he was carrying round and round. He wasn't very old—in his late teens, at her estimation—and that plus the tools he was carrying answered the question for her.

'Are you Maria's son? Riccardo said that he had asked you to do some work in the grounds.'

'*Si, signora.* I am Marco. I am sorry if I have given you the trouble.'

Anna laughed. 'You haven't! Just carry on with whatever you want to do, Marco. I am sure there must be all sorts of work after that storm the other day.'

He frowned deeply. 'There was no storm, *signora*. We have had no storm since the winter—and even then it was just the little one.'

Anna stood quite still, her heart shaking her with its beat. Her hands were clammy with perspiration, yet she felt cold to the tips of her toes. 'Are you sure? I thought that a storm had brought down the telephone lines.'

Marco shrugged, but it was obvious that he had no idea what she was talking about. 'I cannot recall such a happening, *signora*.'

'I see.' She forced herself to smile. 'Then obviously I must have misunderstood. I'll leave you to your work, then, Marco. *Arrivederci.*'

He stood aside while she passed him.

Anna held her head high, her whole body stiff with the restraint she imposed on it. Deep inside a voice was crying, but she didn't dare listen to what it was saying until she had got safely back to the house and shut herself into the bedroom.

She slumped against the wall, so dizzy that for a moment she thought she would fall—but she couldn't give in. She had to make sense of what she'd learned, had to make sense of the fact that Riccardo had lied to her after all. There had been no storm which had brought down the phone lines, she *had* heard the telephone ringing yesterday—even though this morning it hadn't been working. What did it all add up to? What did it mean?

'Why, Ricco?' she whispered. And it seemed to Anna that she had never felt more alone and scared than she did right then in that empty room, with only the lie and Riccardo's deceit for company.

'So, Anna, how was your day?'

She was sitting on the terrace when Riccardo arrived back. She'd heard the car coming up the long, steep climb to the house but hadn't got up to welcome him. She didn't think she could manage that.

Her hands clenched on the smooth cane as she looked up at him and felt her heart ache. Why had he lied to her? What sense had there been in making up that story about the storm? There must have been a reason for it, but all afternoon long she'd failed to find it. Now it lay between them like a barrier she was afraid to cross, but she knew that she had to.

'My day was fine. How did your meeting go?' She wanted to shout the questions at him one after the other, but she held them back, waiting for. . .what? For the answer suddenly to come to her, the simple logical explanation which she had searched for all day long? Or for just another few minutes' grace to sit here and feel her love for this man filling her before she learned why he had chosen to tell her a deliberate lie?

Riccardo gave a heavy sigh, his face grave as he sat down and stretched wearily. 'No better nor worse than I expected.'

'What was it about? Obviously something quite urgent for you to make the journey. Of course, if you could have telephoned then it would have saved you a lot of time. . .but then you couldn't do that, could you, Riccardo? That dreadful storm brought the lines down, didn't it?'

His mouth thinned and he turned to look at her, his silver eyes cold. 'Why do I have the feeling that something is troubling you, Anna?' He gave a short, harsh laugh which sent a shudder running through her because it was so unlike his normal one. 'It appears that your rest has done you less good than I hoped.'

'Then isn't it a pity you didn't take me with you?' She shot to her feet, her face very pale apart from the twin spots of burning colour on each cheekbone. 'If you had then I wouldn't have discovered that there has been no storm. I wouldn't have found out that you, *caro*, have lied to me!'

His face didn't alter. It betrayed nothing of what he was feeling, neither shock nor anger—but then, Riccardo was a master at that, she'd heard. It was only with her that he was open, unguarded, she had always thought—but how wrong she had been, she realised as he sat there now in the chair, so cool and aloof and. . .and distant!

'I suggest you tell me what this is all about, Anna. Then maybe we can sort out this problem you have.'

'Oh, I'm sure we can! I'm sure you will have no difficulty thinking up some other new tale, Ricco, because apparently you are extremely good at that!' She was shaking all over, a fine, tight tension rippling through her in waves, and she heard Riccardo utter something rough as he rose and made as though to take her in his arms, but she stepped away from him at once, unable to bear the thought of him touching her right then.

His hands dropped to his sides, his silver eyes burning with some emotion, but she had no idea what it was. Was it anger or fear which filled them with flames? How could she begin to guess what he felt when it seemed that he had this ability for deceit that she had never suspected before.

'Then perhaps you should tell me just how I have deceived you. Come, Anna, it is obvious that you wish to say something, so let us go inside to the study where we may speak without interruption.'

He gave a thin smile. 'It is a good job I came back when I did, is it not? It seems to me that you have been waiting to get this out into the open for some time.'

He stood aside for her to precede him into the house, impersonally polite as he reached past her to open the study door. Anna walked into the room, glancing back to see Riccardo closing the door behind them. He leant back against it, watching her with hooded eyes which held little expression, that it seemed to Anna that at last she was seeing Riccardo Falcone as others saw him, as the tough, uncompromising man who was held in such awe and even fear by those who worked for him.

'Now, I want to know what this is all about. I come back to my home to be berated for something I do not understand. . .!' He took a deep breath, anger showing in the way he stood there, his hand gripping the brass handle, his powerful body rigid, and for the first time in all her life Anna felt afraid of him.

She turned away, half wishing she had never started this. She didn't want to see Riccardo looking at her like that, didn't want to hear his beautiful voice tainted by anger. What was she doing by destroying their happiness? What purpose would it serve? Yet what purpose had it served Riccardo to tell her a pack of lies?

'Tell me, Anna. I wish to know.'

There was no hint of concession in his deep, dark voice, nothing to make her think that he might be willing to let things drop just to keep the harmony.

Anna felt the first stirrings of doubt. If Riccardo had something to hide then surely he wouldn't be so ready to promote this confrontation?

'Well, Anna, I am waiting.'

He spoke to her with a cool hauteur which set sudden fire to her temper. How dared he speak to her as if she were a naughty child? She had every right in the world to demand an explanation after what had happened today. He was the one who needed to answer a few questions, not she!

She swung round and glared at him. 'I met Marco in the garden this afternoon—'

'Marco?' he interrupted. He frowned heavily before both black brows lifted. 'Maria's son?' At her nod his expression changed, his face turning thunderous. 'And the boy said something to upset you?' When she didn't reply immediately he came to her in swift strides, catching her by the arms before she could escape him, his eyes burning as they searched her face. 'He did not touch you? If he did, then. . .!'

Anna gasped in shock, suddenly realising what he imagined. 'No! Of course not. Don't be ridiculous, Ricco! He was extremely polite and obviously embarrassed that he had disturbed me—although he was simply going about his work as you had told him to.'

'I see. But something did happen to cause you this distress?'

His grip lightened but he still retained his hold on her. Anna could feel the burning imprint of his fingers on her arms and closed her eyes on a sudden wave of pain. Riccardo couldn't have lied to her! It didn't make any sense. Yet the demon inside her wouldn't let it go until she had made him explain.

'I mentioned the storm to Marco, the one you said brought the telephone lines down, and he told me that. . .that there hadn't been any storms since the winter. It was obvious that he had no idea what I was talking about!' She drew away from him, her green eyes blazing into his silver ones, her face very pale now, apart from the twin spots of colour high on each cheekbone.

'And last night, just as I was stepping into the shower, I heard the telephone ringing. So explain it all to me again—about the storm which never was, about the lines which are down and the phone which somehow rings all by itself. . . Tell me, Riccardo, because I need to know!'

There was a long moment of silence, then slowly Riccardo turned and walked across the room. Anna had the feeling that he was withdrawing from her and ached at the thought, but there was little she could do when she so desperately needed answers.

'I am sure that Marco told you the truth as he believes it, Anna. The boy has no reason to lie, although what reason you imagine I have to do so escapes me.' He turned to glance at her then, but there was no warmth in his eyes, none of that tenderness she had always seen before. Riccardo looked at her like a stranger, and her heart broke at the thought, but she met his gaze determinedly.

'That is what I need to know, Ricco. Surely you

can understand that? If you lied to me then why did you do it?'

He held her gaze for a long moment, then turned back to the window almost as though he couldn't bear to look at her any longer. 'Marco and his mother are not from the town. I think I remember telling you that I was lucky to get them to work here at such short notice? I had to apply to an agency and they found them for me. They are from Turin, I believe.'

He swung round, his face betraying nothing now. Anna had never felt as bereft as she did at that moment, seeing such total lack of emotion. 'They arrived the day before we did—several days after the storm had occurred.' He shrugged, but there was nothing forgiving about the look he gave her. 'I do not imagine that they heard about it, let alone witnessed it. However, if you feel the need to have the fact that the storm happened confirmed rather than accept my word for it, then I am sure anyone in the town would be happy to do so. Perhaps we should drive down there now.'

He made it sound so plausible, and made her feel so guilty for ever doubting him, but... 'But what about the telephone I heard ringing. And I did hear it, Riccardo!'

'I am sure you did, Anna. I heard it myself. But when I went to answer it, believing that the lines had been repaired, it was dead.' He gave a smile which held no trace of amusement. 'But you discovered that yourself this morning, did you not? I know little about such matters, but perhaps the engineers were attempting to repair the lines at the time. . .who knows? However, I am sure that it would be possible to find out the answer if it is what you wish. Come.'

He started towards the door, but Anna made no move to follow him. Her head was reeling with what he had told her, her heart heavy with the realisation of what she had done. It was all so simple. Every word that Riccardo had said to her made such sense, and every single doubt she'd had all day long made none! Why on earth had she imagined that Riccardo had lied to her? Suddenly her own stupidity seemed beyond belief.

'Well, Anna, do you not wish to ask your questions?'

'No. I don't need to.' She looked away, her voice husky with the tears she was holding back. 'I'm sorry, Ricco. I know it isn't enough, but I am sorry for ever doubting you.'

There was a moment when he didn't speak, when the silence hung between them, then he gave a weary sigh. 'I have doubted myself many times, Anna, but the only thing I can say with all sincerity is that I shall never, in this life or beyond, do anything to harm you!'

'Riccardo, I . . .!'

Her voice echoed back at her because Riccardo had gone. Anna closed her eyes on a wave of bitter regret. It had been her own insecurity which had scored this wound in their happiness. Now she knew that it would be hard to help it heal.

* * *

Riccardo was waiting in the dining room when Anna came downstairs that night. She hadn't seen him since they had spoken in the study. He had used the small dressing room next to their bedroom to shower and change, and that in itself had seemed like an omen.

She stopped on the rug so that he wouldn't hear her footsteps until she had herself under control, but it was hard to control the sudden flood of memories of all the other nights they had gone to their room to change for dinner and ended up in bed together. She could recall it all so clearly, the way they had laughingly rushed afterwards to get ready in time to eat the meal served in the elegant dining room with its cut crystal and exquisite porcelain.

Anna closed her eyes as the memories seeped into her mind one after the other, recalling the tender touch of hands across the table, the looks which had made their blood heat again. . .

'*Signora*?'

She started nervously, colouring when she found Maria watching her. What must the poor woman be thinking, finding her mooning about like this? Anna cleared her throat, making an effort to sound in control, but the fear about what harm she might have done with her silly insecurities was still inside her. 'Yes, Maria. Did you wish to speak to me?'

'*Si.*' The woman twisted her starched white apron, looking ill at ease. 'It is my boy—my Marco. He did not mean to cause the trouble. I would be so. . . so. . .' The word she wanted eluded her and she shrugged. 'Marco is to go to the university this year. He studies the English, *si*?'

Anna nodded, wondering where all this was leading to. She glanced into the dining room, feeling colour coming into her face as she saw Riccardo watching her. She turned away at once, unsure how to handle that searching look.

It was odd, but at times lately she found it hard to understand what Riccardo was thinking, yet before she had never had any difficulty. Was the change in him or her? Had her perception of him altered in some way, and was it that which was making the difference? Either answer worried her, because she wanted everything to be just as it had before. . .

'*Signora*?'

'That is wonderful for him, Maria. You must be very proud,' she replied distractedly.

The woman's face lit up. 'I am. . .very proud of my Marco. But he cannot go if he has not enough money, you understand? To work here for the *signore* means that Marco can make his studies. That is why I took the job, even though I was not sure—'

She stopped abruptly, her lined face colouring before she looked down at the floor. Anna had a feeling that Maria regretted something she had said, but couldn't work out what. But still, she had her own problems to contend with without adding that to them.

'I understand, Maria. But if it is an increase in salary you are asking for I am afraid you must speak to Signor Falcone about it.'

'No! The money I am to be paid is good. I am happy with it. But if Marco has not the job. . .'

She shrugged, obviously embarrassed, but suddenly Anna understood. She glanced into the dining room again, but Riccardo was nowhere in sight now. Had Riccardo been so angry about what had happened that he had threatened Marco with dismissal?

Anna knew it was the answer and her temper surged to life. It wasn't fair that the boy should suffer for her mistakes! She turned back to Maria and smiled, but there was a spark in her green eyes now.

'I see no reason why Marco should not continue his job, Maria. It is obvious that he is a nice boy and a conscientious worker. I shall make sure that Signor Falcone knows that.'

Maria nodded, smiling in relief as she murmured her thanks, but Anna had already turned away. She walked into the dining room, the light of battle in her eyes as she took her place at the table before Riccardo could pull out her chair with his usual courtesy.

His eyebrows lifted fractionally, but he made no comment as Maria carried in the soup and waited attentively on Anna before leaving the room again. Riccardo watched her go, then looked at Anna with a wry smile.

'You seem to have reached an understanding with Maria, then?'

Anna tasted the delicious soup before answering, although if she'd been asked what flavour it was she would have been hard pressed to say. 'Yes. It wasn't hard. Any woman could understand her concern for her son.'

Riccardo said nothing, merely drank his soup, leaving her to elaborate or not as she chose, and Anna felt her temper rise another notch at his arrogance. 'Did you threaten Marco because he spoke to me before?'

He broke off a piece of roll but made no attempt to eat it. 'I find it unnecessary to threaten employees, Anna.'

Arrogant didn't even begin to describe him! Her green eyes sparkled but she made herself speak calmly. 'I'm sure you don't. People always do as you tell them without the need for threats—isn't that right, Riccardo?'

He put down the bread. 'Why not simply tell me what is troubling you now, *cara*. That way perhaps we can enjoy our meal in peace.'

He made her sound once again like a child throwing a tantrum, and the thought infuriated her. 'Very well. I don't think it fair that Marco should be blamed for my foolishness. Evidently this job means a lot to him, and without it he will not be able to go to university this autumn. He didn't say anything out of turn. It was just me putting my own. . .own stupid construction on things which caused the problem!'

Riccardo shrugged. 'Perhaps the problem was there before?'

'I don't know what you mean.'

'No? It is obvious that you must have been having doubts, and that is why you went to the study this morning to see if the telephone was working. What I cannot understand is why you simply did not mention hearing it last night?'

He was justified in asking that, but Anna found it impossible to explain the uncertainty she'd felt. It seemed ridiculous now that Riccardo had explained everything so simply, but the doubts had been very real at the time. She stayed silent and heard him give a harsh laugh.

'Perhaps there are other things bothering you though, Anna—not only the telephone which rings when it should not do so. Maybe you should tell me about those as well?'

Her face flamed at his sarcasm but she forced herself to meet his challenging stare as levelly as she could. 'All right then, Riccardo, seeing as you ask. It struck me today just how little I know about your business. Why is that?'

'I have no idea.' He shrugged, but there was a tightness to his mouth suddenly, a grim cast to his features which made Anna wonder if she had gone too far. 'However, if there is something you wish to know, then ask, Anna. I have no secrets I wish to keep from you. Perhaps you should have started asking these questions some time ago, though. It seems to me that the accident cannot be solely responsible for all your present uncertainties about me.'

His gaze was searching, almost too intent, but suddenly Anna decided that she wasn't going to compound one mistake with another. Things were getting out of hand. Riccardo had never seemed as distant as he did right now, and she hated it. She loved him; she didn't want to quarrel with him when there was no need. The thought cooled her temper just as quickly as it had heated.

'But I didn't have any doubts, Ricco. I have never had any doubts about the fact that I love you.' She touched his hand where it lay on the white tablecloth, praying that he would accept the gesture as it was meant. 'I can't explain properly, probably can't make you understand how I feel, but losing my memory has made me unsure of *myself*—and that is what is causing the trouble. I keep imagining all sorts of crazy things simply because I can't remember the past and what happened.'

She willed him to understand and felt her heart lift when he turned his hand over and captured hers.

'I do understand, Anna. I understand how confused you must feel, how unsure, but you need have no doubts about how I feel. I love you more than life itself, and never in any way would I set out to hurt you.'

'Oh, Ricco!' On a sudden impulse she bent towards him and kissed him, feeling his mouth warm against hers. She drew back and smiled at him, watching the flames which sprang to life in his silver eyes, understanding them so well. This was all that mattered—their love. The rest could never touch them.

'The accident was a great shock, Anna. But in time you will put it into perspective.'

'I know. If only I could remember all these niggling little details, though, it would be so much easier! My mind runs riot at times, picking up on small, insignificant things to go racing off at a tangent!'

'It is understandable, *cara*. Why, even Dr Lewis warned that it would take time before you are fully yourself again.'

'Yes, I know, but I don't think I realised in the hospital just how much of my memory is missing.' She gave a soft little laugh, realising that Riccardo did understand how she felt. She should have known that he would because he had always understood her—almost better than she had understood herself at times!

'If only we could flick a switch and play back the past year as though it was a film then we could pick up the pieces of our life exactly where we left off.'

Something flashed across his face, but then he caught her hand and carried it to his mouth to press the lightest of kisses to the back of it, yet Anna felt the sensations ripple through every pulse-point.

'We cannot go back, Anna. We must look to the future. It seems unnecessary to my mind that you should keep torturing yourself by trying to recall what is over and done with when there is so much else to look forward to. Surely the fact that you are safe and well and that we have one another is more than enough to build our happiness on?'

'It is, of course. You're right, darling. I am being silly. I can't even understand why I'm doing it. It isn't as though I have forgotten anything really important!'

It was wonderful to see the warmth in his eyes

again, to see the tenderness in the look he gave her. Just being deprived of it for a short while made her realise how precious it was. She needed Riccardo so much! He was the man she loved, the man she wanted to spend the whole of her life with. She couldn't bear to find out anything about him which would change that.

The thought came from nowhere, as though a door had opened briefly then slammed shut again. Anna felt as though she had been given a glimpse of some dark nightmare waiting in the shadows and shuddered.

'Anna?'

Riccardo's voice sounded concerned, and she fought free of the shadows, chased them away with the brilliance of their love. There could be nothing about Riccardo's life that she would hate to find out. It was just another of those demons let loose to torment her, but she wouldn't allow this one to do any damage as the others had.

She gave him a brilliant smile, rubbing her cheek against his hand. 'I'm fine now. It. . .it just struck me how easily I could have damaged our relationship with my foolishness.'

'Our love for one another will stand any test, Anna, I hope.'

His silver eyes burned as they met hers in a look which was suddenly too searching, and what had sounded at first like a statement ended as a need for reassurance.

Anna took a deep breath and murmured something which was obviously appropriate, because

Riccardo smiled and turned the topic along other less fraught channels. But although Anna responded to him on one level, on another she could still feel that strange sense of unease nagging away at her, that old demon joining forces with the new.

Riccardo was a man who made things happen the way he wanted them to. His self-assurance was legendary, yet for that fleeting moment she had looked at him and seen uncertainty—and that made her feel afraid. *Did* Riccardo know something that might affect how she felt about him? Or was she merely being fanciful again?

CHAPTER FIVE

THE sky was clear and blue the next morning, with the promise of another glorious day ahead. Anna poured coffee into the huge white breakfast cups for her and Riccardo, then took a sip of the fragrant brew, wishing that she felt more like enjoying the wonderful weather. Once again she hadn't slept well, and when she had finally drifted off she had been haunted by dreams that she couldn't recall now but which had left behind a lingering sadness that she couldn't shake off.

'You are very quiet this morning, *cara.* You are feeling well, I hope?'

Riccardo set down his cup, concern etched on his face as he studied her, and Anna had no difficulty in smiling at him. He looked so handsome sitting there, the breeze blowing his black hair across his forehead, the white polo shirt such a startling contrast against his tanned skin. He had left it open at the neck, and, unbidden, her eyes travelled down the length of his strong throat. She felt her pulse leap slightly as her senses stirred. She loved him so much! Life without Riccardo would be unbearable, but then she would never need to be without him... would she?

The demon awoke again and touched her happiness, but she held the smile, not wanting it to touch

Riccardo. Once the telephone lines were restored she intended to put a call through to Dr Lewis and ask him if these feelings she was having were normal. It seemed like a simple explanation, of course, that losing her memory had placed these doubts in her mind. Dr Lewis would probably confirm that most sufferers of the condition felt as she did—a little unsure, a little afraid that there was something waiting in the background to spring at her.

'I'm fine, darling. Was I miles away?' She feigned a light laugh to cover the moment. 'I was just thinking how handsome you look and how much I would like to paint your portrait. Will you sit for me this morning?'

'If it is what you wish, but first I must drive down to the town. There is a call I need to make, some letters which must be posted.' He smiled and pressed her back into the seat as she made to rise. 'No, you stay and enjoy your breakfast, Anna. It will take me less than an hour, then I will be back and yours to do with as you wish.'

His deep voice turned the softly teasing statement into a sensual promise, and Anna coloured delicately, hearing Riccardo's soft laugh as he bent to kiss her lightly on the lips. They had slept side by side in the huge brass bed beneath the starched white sheets which smelled of pine, but Riccardo had made no attempt to make love to her and strangely Anna had felt no desire for him to do so. Now, though, she felt her desire for him rise so swiftly that she could feel it throbbing in every cell.

She looked up at him and saw on his face an echo of what she was feeling, this deep, unremitting passion. It comforted her, because while they felt this way about one another then nothing had changed. It was a sweet reminder of the way they had fallen in love—so quickly, so devastatingly.

Her mind drifted back as she listened to the throb of the engine as Riccardo drove away from the villa, back to those glorious days when Riccardo's love had first filled her whole world. . .

'It is beautiful, Riccardo! I don't think I have ever seen anything so lovely.' Anna held up the delicate mist of veil, watching the way the tiny seed pearls sewn into its folds glowed in the sunlight.

'I am glad you like it, my darling. It would give me great pleasure if you would wear it at our wedding.' Riccardo drew her to him and kissed her gently, his face full of love. 'It belonged to my mother, and to her mother before that.'

Anna kissed him back, wondering what she had done to deserve such happiness. It had all happened so fast, falling in love with Riccardo and agreeing to marry him, but she had no doubts that it was what she wanted. The wedding was set for just a week's time at the small church in the town, and she could hardly wait for the day to come when she would be Riccardo's wife.

'I shall cherish it, Ricco. I only wish your mother could be there to see me wearing it.'

'I wish she could too, but as I explained, Anna, she rarely leaves her home in Palermo now. The journey would be too tiring for her.' He shrugged, but there was an odd expression on his face as he drew away from her and stared across the sweep of the gardens towards the olive grove.

Anna shivered, suddenly chilled, although she couldn't have explained why. It was just that Riccardo looked so distant. . .

She put her hand gently on his arm, understanding why immediately. 'I know you will miss not having her there, darling, but we can visit her after the honeymoon. Are you sure there is nobody else you wish to ask?' She gave a gentle laugh, loving him for his consideration. 'You mustn't think that you can't ask anyone you want to just because I'll have no one at the wedding apart from Nell. I've already told you that now Grandma is dead I don't have any close relatives, so our situation isn't quite the same.'

'Indeed it isn't!' He turned and captured her hand, laughing into her eyes. 'I have so many aunts and uncles and cousins that I could fill the church twice over, *cara*! But to invite one means I must invite them all, and that is not what I want. All I want is you there on the day we pledge our love for one another.'

'Oh, Ricco, that's just how I feel! And it's going to be the most perfect day. Nell has nearly finished my dress and it's just how I wanted it to look.'

She smiled happily, thinking of the fine white cotton voile which her friend had skilfully fashioned into a simple gown which skimmed Anna's slender body as it fell from a high neckline to her ankles. It made her look young and virginal, and for a dubious moment Anna wondered if it might not be sophisticated enough—even though she knew she'd looked beautiful when she had tried it on.

'I hope you like it, Riccardo,' she said hesitantly. 'I know you wanted to buy me a designer gown, but. . .'

'But you prefer your independence and to choose the gown yourself. I understand, Anna, and I love you because of it. It is what makes you the woman you are. And I know that you will look beautiful and that our wedding day will be a day I shall remember all my life.' He kissed her hand, his cool lips lingering against her skin. 'To have you for my wife, Anna, is all I want. I need nothing and no one else, and never shall. . .'

Anna shivered as the sun slid behind a cloud, leaving the terrace suddenly overcast. Odd that she should recall that conversation she and Riccardo had had—odder still that it should leave behind this unsettling feeling that something wasn't quite right.

She searched her mind and realised what was causing it. She still hadn't met Riccardo's mother, or any other of his numerous relatives. There had never seemed to be enough time to make the journey to Palermo where most of them lived. Now it struck her as strange that Riccardo hadn't made the time to do so. It was almost as though he didn't want her to meet his family. . .

Anna got up from the table, determinedly putting that fanciful notion out of her head. Riccardo was a very busy man, as she knew only too well; he couldn't just take off and leave his business. Why, even today he had needed to attend to something or other. It was just that her thoughts seemed to have a life of their own lately, latching onto the most ridiculously inconsequential ideas and making mountainous molehills out of them! What she needed to do was to focus on something positive, and what better than the portrait she intended painting of Riccardo?

She started back inside, then stopped when she heard a car. Riccardo couldn't be back so soon, surely? Curious, she walked around the front of the villa and stopped in the shadows of a tall cypress tree to watch as an unfamiliar car drew up in the drive and a stranger got out. He glanced round, then saw her standing by the house.

'Hello?'

He spoke English, and that surprised her so much that for a moment she just stood and stared at him. He gave a wry laugh.

'Well, it can't be my stunning good looks which have stolen your tongue, so it must be the fact you don't speak English.' He smiled again, his eyes reflecting appreciation as they skimmed over her before he broke into stilted Italian.

'There's no need.' Anna stopped him with an apologetic laugh. 'I'm sorry—I was just surprised to see you, and even more surprised to realise you are English. We get few English visitors up here, you see.'

'Well, thank heavens for that!' At her obvious lack of comprehension he continued with a grin,

'My Italian is somewhat limited, and holding a conversation can only be classed as a strain!'

Anna laughed again. 'I know what you mean. Despite living here for over a year now I'm still not fluent.' She held her hand out. 'I'm Anna Falcone.'

The man's shock was obvious. 'Riccardo's wife?' He took her outstretched hand, holding it just a moment longer than poilteness dictated before he let it go. 'I knew he was married, of course. I read about it in the papers a couple of years ago now.'

Anna shook her head. 'No, we've been married just over a year, Mr. . .?'

'Grady, Patrick Grady.' He seemed to hesitate. 'And you say that you and Riccardo have been married how long? A year?'

'Yes.' She frowned. 'You look puzzled, Mr Grady. Why?'

'Oh, no reason at all. I just thought that you'd been married longer than that, but obviously I must have got my facts wrong. I haven't seen Riccardo in some time,' he finished smoothly.

'And I'm afraid he isn't here at the moment. He's driven into town but he won't be long. Perhaps I can offer you a drink . . .?' She stopped at the sound of a car engine. 'That sounds like him coming back now, in fact.'

They stood side by side, waiting until the car turned onto the gravel driveway. Riccardo brought it to an abrupt halt, his eyes narrowing as he jumped out and came towards them. Anna had the sudden feeling that he wasn't pleased, but had no idea why.

'Patrick, I didn't expect to see you here.' He held his hand out, his face betraying little.

Patrick Grady shook it, an edge to his voice. 'I rather guessed that. However, your message was relayed to me by my office, so I thought it simpler to drive over. I'm staying a few miles away at Greve.'

'I see. Then I appreciate you taking the trouble.' Riccardo glanced at Anna, his face softening as he slid an arm around her shoulders. 'You and Patrick have introduced yourselves, I hope, *cara*.'

'Of course—although I have a bone to pick with you. Patrick seems to believe that you and I have been married for two years. So come clean, Ricco, what aren't you telling me?'

He stiffened at once, the hand clasping her shoulder tightening until she gave a small murmur of pain. He apologised at once, but his face was set when he glanced at the other man, his eyes holding what seemed to Anna to be a warning. 'I cannot imagine how Patrick made such a mistake, but neither can I imagine what you think I might be hiding, *cara*.'

Anna slid from his hold, forcing a smile. Had she imagined that look Riccardo had given the other man? Maybe, but she hadn't imagined the way his hand had fastened on her so tightly that she would have a bruise later. What was the matter? She couldn't work it out, and in the end merely dismissed the incident as lightly as she could.

'Oh, I suppose it did cross my mind that you might have another wife tucked away some place.'

Riccardo laughed deeply, his face smoothing out. 'I do not think I would need another wife when I have you, my darling. You are more than enough for me.' He glanced at Grady. 'Shall we go into the study, Patrick?'

'Of course.' Grady turned to Anna. 'It was good to meet you, Mrs Falcone.'

'And you, Mr Grady. But I was just offering you a drink, wasn't I?' She looked at Riccardo. 'Shall I bring some to the study for both of you?'

'Do not trouble yourself, Anna. I am sure Patrick has many things he needs to do and does not wish to be delayed here for too long.'

Riccardo led the way into the house with the other man following. Anna watched them go, then took a deep breath, feeling the shadows closing in on her again. Another demon, another piece to be fitted into the puzzle—but where and how did Patrick Grady fit in?

'You're wrong, Riccardo! Completely wrong. She should know the truth.'

'That is my decision, my friend.'

Riccardo's tone was icy and Anna stopped dead in her tracks. She hadn't meant to eavesdrop, but she'd been passing the study just as the men had raised their voices. She paused for a moment, her heart beating a shade faster. What were they discussing? It made no sense, yet Anna had the sudden feeling that she was the person Grady had referred to. What had he meant, that she should know the truth? The truth about what? Obviously something which had displeased Riccardo, if that hard note in his voice was anything to go by.

She jumped as the door suddenly opened, but it was too late to move away. Riccardo caught sight of her at once and frowned before he forced a smile as he came to her.

'Were you wondering what was keeping us, Anna?' He took her hand and kissed it lightly, but his silver eyes were searching, and with a sudden insight Anna knew that he was wondering how much of the conversation she had overheard.

She returned his smile, not quite meeting his eyes as she uttered the small white lie, and wondered why she should feel the need to do so. 'Of course not. I'd just come along the hall when I heard the door opening, so I thought I'd see if Mr Grady would care to stay for lunch.'

Patrick Grady smiled, but his eyes were troubled as they rested on her. 'Thank you, but no. Unfortunately I do have another appointment, which means I shall have to leave immediately.' He glanced at Riccardo, and a look passed between them. 'I shall be in touch, Riccardo. Leave it with me. I shall do all I can, but please think about what I said. You could be doing more harm than good, even with the best of intentions.'

Riccardo stiffened, his face faintly arrogant. 'I know what I am doing, Patrick.'

Grady shrugged. 'Then I only hope it works out in the end. I shall speak to you as soon as I hear anything.'

With another polite smile at Anna he left, and

after a second or so they heard the sound of his car. Anna let out the pent up breath she hadn't even known she was holding and glanced at Riccardo.

'Your Mr Grady sounded very serious just now. Is there something wrong, Riccardo?'

'Of course not. Just some minor business matter which Patrick is helping me with.' He bent and kissed her, his lips as warm and tender as ever, but for once the magic of his touch left Anna unmoved.

She drew away, avoiding the faintly quizzical look he gave her as she walked swiftly to the stairs. 'If you don't mind, Riccardo, I think I shall lie down for an hour before lunch. I feel rather tired this morning.'

'Of course you must. You have been doing too much, *cara*. You must remember that you are not fully recovered yet.'

She gave him a brittle smile. 'I thought you kept telling me that I have remembered all I need to.'

'I meant, of course, that you are not fully recovered from the physical injuries.'

His tone was sharp, and Anna felt suddenly weary of all the pretence. She turned and hurried up the stairs to their room. Walking to the window, she opened the shutters and stared across the rolling green hills, wondering when she and Riccardo had first begun fencing with words. In the past it had been so easy to tell him everything which troubled her. . .apart from her one big fear.

The door in her memory opened again, and once again her mind recoiled from what it might learn. Anna felt tears brimming in her eyes. She could tell herself a hundred times that everything was all right, but in her heart she knew that it wasn't.

There was something in the past she hadn't remembered—something so dark and terrifying that her mind had shut it out because it affected her love for Riccardo.

'Anna, darling, what is it?'

He had moved so softly as he crossed the room and slid his arms around her to draw her back against his powerful body that Anna started the fear running through her so swiftly that it made her gasp.

'*Cara*, it is me!' He turned her round, tilting her face to stare into her haunted green eyes, smoothing the tears from her cheeks with his thumbs. 'Tell me, Anna, what makes you cry like this? What causes such unhappiness?'

She pressed her head into his shoulder, wanting to tell him more than anything, yet not knowing what to say. And somehow he guessed.

'It is some ghost from the past, is it not? Something you are starting to remember?'

'Yes. It's there, Ricco, like a dark shade, and it scares me! Do you know what it is? Can you tell me?' She clung to him in sudden urgency, her hands clasping the smooth white cotton of his shirt, her fingers cold. 'I think I shall go mad if I don't get answers soon. I... I overheard you and Patrick Grady talking—something about "she should know the truth". Was it me you were speaking about? Tell me, Riccardo, please, because if there is something I should know then I want to hear it!'

Riccardo murmured something soft and tender,

his hand gentle as he cradled her head against him. 'I have been trying to spare you the unhappiness, Anna, but perhaps I was wrong.' He seemed to hesitate, his chest rising and falling swiftly, his voice grating with an emotion so raw that Anna felt it in every cell. 'We were to have a child, *cara*, but. . .but it was not to be in the end.'

He raised her face to look deep into her shocked green eyes. 'You had a miscarriage, Anna, and our baby died.'

'I. . .' She couldn't seem to find any words. There were none to make sense of what Riccardo had told her. She stood there staring into his eyes and waited for her mind to release its secret, waited to feel the pain she must surely feel, but she felt nothing. She had no memory of the child nor of losing it—no memory of something so important that it would have changed both her life and Riccardo's irrevocably!

'I. . . I can't remember.' Her voice was no more than a horrified whisper. 'I can't remember our baby, Ricco!'

'Shhh! I should not have told you. You were not ready for it. When you are able to cope then you will remember.' His deep voice broke on a note of pain and Anna felt wetness on her cheek, not from her own tears but from his.

She held him close, crying with him, but her tears were for her lack of memories and his were because the memory of their loss was so bitter. A child. She let the thought sink into her mind, trying to recall what she must have felt at the time—the joy which knowing she was carrying Riccardo's baby would have brought her, the searing sense of loss when she had lost it later—but her mind and body were blank. She could understand Riccardo's pain yet she couldn't share it, couldn't grieve for this child she didn't remember.

He drew back slowly, then turned away from her, almost as though he was ashamed that she should have witnessed his anguish, but Anna touched his arm. 'I wish I could remember, Riccardo. I cannot understand why I don't. To have your child was always my dearest wish, yet I feel nothing! Why?'

'Because your mind knows that it would be too much for you to cope with, I imagine. Dr Lewis told me that it is impossible to rush these things.'

He pushed his hands into his pockets, his wide shoulders hunched, his silver eyes more like pewter, tinged with the memories she couldn't share. What must it have been like for Riccardo, living with this grief yet unable to share it with her, afraid in case it caused her more distress? It seemed to Anna that it proved once again how much he loved her.

'When did it happen? Did I lose the baby because of the accident or...?' She didn't finish but he answered the question anyway.

'No, it happened some time before your accident, Anna. That was not to blame for it.'

There was something utterly weary in his tone that she couldn't understand—until it came to her in a flash of bitter insight that he blamed himself in some way. 'How did it happen? Tell me, Ricco. I might not remember, but I want to know.' She touched a hand lightly to her flat stomach, wondering how it had felt to know that she was carrying Riccardo's child below her heart.

Something crossed his face and his jaw tightened, but his voice was almost too level. Riccardo was afraid of upsetting her and suffering because of it. She took his hand between both of hers, her eyes loving, and heard him sigh.

'It happened one night at our house in Milan. I. . .I was not there at the time, Anna, and I shall blame myself always for that. When I came home and found you it was already too late to save the baby.'

'I'm so sorry,' she whispered. 'Even though I cannot remember I know I would have loved it with all my heart because it was your child, Ricco. . .the child our love had created.' She stopped, struck by a sudden cold thought. 'Af—after the miscarriage what did the doctors say, Riccardo? Can I still have children or. . .'

She couldn't go on, but Riccardo drew her to him, holding her tightly. 'Yes! You can have other children, Anna. There was no damage done by the miscarriage. Please do not torture yourself by thinking that, *cara mia*!'

Anna gasped. 'I was so afraid. . .so scared that that was something else I couldn't remember!'

'Then there is no need. When the time is right then you will have another child, *cara*.' He brushed her mouth with a gentle kiss, his eyes holding a wealth of tenderness.

Anna smiled, letting the warmth flow back into her cold body. It had been a shock, and she guessed that it would hurt more rather than less as the days passed and she got used to the idea. But the thought that she could have another child was a comfort. It must be a comfort to Riccardo too, because she had seen how stricken he still was by their loss. Maybe a baby was what they needed—something to focus their future on?

She tipped her head back and looked deep into his eyes, 'And what if I told you that I would like a baby soon, Ricco?'

He stiffened before slowly he set her away from him and walked over to the window. 'It would not be a good idea, Anna. Not yet.'

What was there in his voice which took the warmth and turned it back to ice? Anna stood where she was, her eyes locked to his broad back as she felt the chill seep through to her soul. 'Why? Why wouldn't it be a good idea? Tell me, Riccardo.'

He swung round, his face partly shadowed so that it was impossible to read his expression clearly. 'Because you need time to recover from the ordeal of the accident.' He shrugged, but his tone was guarded. 'Dr Lewis advised against such things for a while.'

'Did he, indeed? Well, it seems to me that good old Dr Lewis thought of everything! Mind you, one follows on from the other, I imagine; Dr Lewis doesn't want us sleeping together, so that in itself should negate the possibility of a child!'

Anna couldn't explain why she was suddenly

angry. Perhaps it was just that she was sick and tired of being told what was good for her. What possible bar could there be to her getting pregnant? The operation had been a success and her other injuries had almost healed; she was in better physical shape than many women! But had Dr Lewis been more concerned with her mental state rather than her physical one? Was there something he knew which had made him level such a warning?

'Anna, I—'

'No, please don't say anything more.' She cut him off, not wanting to hear any more placating words. If there was something wrong she needed to know about it—the same way she needed to know everything that had happened in the past. Riccardo might be trying to spare her the pain, but it wasn't what she wanted. She had to know it all so that she could make her own judgements, although she guessed that Riccardo wouldn't like the idea. 'I'm sorry. What you told me was a shock, Riccardo, but I apologise for acting the way I just did.'

'*Cara*, it does not matter. I understand.'

He came and took her in his arms, holding her close, murmuring to her in soft Italian, but the words made no impression, his touch even less, and her heart ached at the thought. She wanted to stand in Riccardo's arms and feel her blood heat, feel the passion rise so swiftly, because only then would she feel completely alive.

Yet she stood there now, her heart empty, her body a dark void, the future stretching before her in a sea of loneliness. And she made herself a silent promise that somehow, some way she would open that door to her memory. . .no matter what she discovered on the other side.

CHAPTER SIX

It wasn't in Anna's nature to be devious, and keeping up the pretence that everything was fine in front of Riccardo was a strain, but it was the only way, she sensed, to achieve her objective. Riccardo could so easily reason away her fears when he was with her, but that wasn't the answer. She had to vanquish them herself by finding out what was behind them.

The thought of how she could make herself remember what had happened in the past nagged at her like a painful ache which nothing would soothe. Her mind kept worrying at the problem but the answer eluded her. She was surrounded by familiar things, in a place where she had spent so many happy days, yet nothing happened. It was over lunch a few days later that it suddenly struck her what the answer was.

Anna felt the shock run through her in cold little waves, stunned by her own blindness. But had it been less that than her mind deliberately keeping the door tightly closed? She picked up her glass and took a long drink of the iced water, feeling its coolness inching its way down a throat which was parched and choked with nerves.

The secret lay in the house in Milan. How she

knew that she had no idea, but suddenly it was there in her mind, as cold and as clear as the water.

'So, *cara*, what shall we do this afternoon? Do you wish to paint for a while? There is some paperwork I need to do if you are to be busy.'

Anna jumped, spilling the glass of water, guilt at what she was planning making her nervous. 'Oh, heavens. Look what I've done!'

She shot to her feet, mopping at the pool of water with her linen napkin, then stopped abruptly with colour in her cheeks when Riccardo caught her hand, his gaze searching.

'Leave it. Maria will attend to it. What is wrong, Anna? You have been acting strangely for the past few days.' There was a sudden anguish in his eyes as they held hers. 'Is it what I told you about the baby?'

Anna looked away, hating herself for the lie she must tell—although the baby and her inability to remember it was all part and parcel of the problem. How did she know that Riccardo would refuse to let her confront those ghosts from her past? She had no idea, but she had to discover the truth. If she could forget about the baby then what else could she have forgotten?

'It. . .it was a shock.'

'*Cara*. . .' He drew her to him, his arms around her waist as he pulled her down onto his lap and pressed kisses to her temple. Even in the week they had been here her hair had grown, and the silky curls gave her the look of an angel as they floated around her head. He smoothed his hand over them, smiling as they twined around his long fingers. 'You must not distress yourself. I blame myself for telling you. Seeing your sad eyes haunts me.'

'I had to know, Riccardo.' She lifted suddenly urgent green eyes to his. 'Can you understand that, darling? I need to know everything, no matter how painful it is.'

His face grew shuttered. 'I can understand your frustration, Anna, but it could be dangerous to rush things before you are ready.'

'Rush things!' She gave a brittle little laugh which carried through the clear, still air almost like a challenge, and Riccardo's eyes narrowed.

'*Si.* It is only a matter of weeks since your accident.'

'And that's weeks too long!' She got to her feet, suddenly needing to make him understand this urgency, wanting him to help her. 'Can you imagine what it is like, Riccardo, *knowing* that there are parts of your life that you have totally forgotten? You look at me and see the woman you fell in love with, the woman you married, but I'm not her any longer. I'm just a pale reflection of myself, and I won't be anything else until all the missing links are joined and the past meshes with the present without gaps!'

'You are no pale reflection, *cara*.'

He rose to his feet, his eyes lingering on her angry figure in the floating floral dress of mauves and pinks. With its tiny cap-sleeves and long, flowing skirt it was an intensely feminine dress and Anna saw his eyes darken, yet surprisingly she felt nothing.

Since the day when she had learned about the baby and realised how much she must have forgotten she'd felt drained of all emotions. Now, as Riccardo came to her, she stepped aside.

'No! That isn't the answer.' She gave a harsh little laugh. 'Sorry, Riccardo, but you aren't going to throw me off track today with a few kisses!'

She could hardly believe she had said that. She heard the words, felt the shock which followed in their wake—both Riccardo's shock and her own. She had never spoken to him that way before, never rejected him, never wanted to, and it was as though suddenly a huge chasm opened beneath their feet.

He stared her down, his silver eyes like ice. 'It seems to me that by reaching into the past you are destroying the future. Which is the more important to you, Anna? This need to know all the unimportant details from the past or our life together now?'

'The baby can hardly be classed as unimportant, Ricco! Can't you understand that I am terrified? That learning I had forgotten our child means that I could have forgotten so many other things as well!'

She took a deep breath, desperate to make him understand, wanting with all her heart to have Riccardo beside her in this terrifying battle rather than against her. 'If there was anything else, anything like the baby, then promise me that you would have told me.'

He stared at her for one long moment which seemed like an eternity, his voice grating when he finally answered. 'Do you need to ask that, Anna? Do you no longer trust me to care for your welfare?'

He laughed bitterly, his eyes like twin shards of ice, his handsome face set—Riccardo Falcone at his most dauntingly arrogant! 'When you can give *me* the answer to those questions then perhaps you will answer your own!'

He turned and strode back inside the house without waiting for her to say anything. Anna sank down onto a chair, shaking all over from that bitter confrontation. She and Riccardo had quarrelled in the past, but never like that. Never had he looked at her as though she had betrayed him, and the memory of it hurt so much that she wanted to rush after him and sort it out, yet something held her back—that demon again, poisoning her mind with doubts. Riccardo hadn't answered her question. Why? Because he couldn't swear with hand on heart that he had told her everything?

Anna ran a hand over her throbbing forehead, feeling the tight band of pain around her temples. Only, it seemed, by finding out the truth, whether. . . whether Riccardo had told her everything, would she be freed from this never-ending nightmare.

'*Signora*, you are not well? I must call Signor Falcone, *si*?'

Maria half turned to rush back inside the house, but Anna stopped her. She didn't think she could take another confrontation just yet. She needed time to think, space to let her mind rove through the possibilities. Riccardo couldn't or wouldn't give her either of those.

'No!' She softened her tone at the woman's start of surprise. 'There is no need to call my husband,

Maria. He is busy, and it is just a slight headache, that is all.' She got up, picking up the straw sun hat from where it lay on a chair and putting it on to shade her face from the glare. 'I think I shall go for a walk. If my husband asks tell him that I won't be long, please.'

'*Si, signora*, and thank you.'

Anna glanced back, her face faintly puzzled. 'I'm sorry, but I'm not sure what you mean.'

There was a flush of excitement on the woman's lined face. 'Signor Falcone told my Marco that he will be his. . .his. . .' She struggled to find the word, lifting her hands helplessly at her inability. 'Signor Falcone will pay the money for Marco to go to his studies in the university. But it is thanks to you, *signora. Grazie—grazie tanto!*'

Anna held the smile, murmuring what she hoped was appropriate before making her way from the terrace. Tears were misting her eyes but she blinked them away. Riccardo had had no need to make such an offer, but he had done so because of her. He had listened to her pleas for Marco and in his usual generous way had done more than he had needed to because he had known it would please her. Yet all she did was repay his love with doubts. Riccardo deserved more from her than that. . .so much more!

It was cool amongst the trees, but when Anna stepped out onto the road a little lower down the hill the sun beat down on her bare arms. For a moment she hesitated, wondering if she should turn back and try to make her peace with Riccardo, but he had mentioned something about paperwork and she didn't think it fair to disturb him. Obviously this problem with the business hadn't been resolved, which was why he had contacted Patrick Grady, although she couldn't guess how the Englishman could help.

Musing idly on it, she made her way slowly towards the town, feeling more at peace than she had felt in days. Seeing Riccardo suddenly for what he was—a caring, conscientious man—made her fears seem ridiculous. If there had been anything at all he'd thought she should know then Riccardo would have told her when he had told her about the baby.

The town was quiet when Anna arrived. She looked longingly at the café on the corner of the piazza, but she hadn't brought any money with her to buy a cup of coffee so she carried on along the street. In the past year the area had become increasingly popular with English tourists, and one of the shops even had a few English newspapers on show.

Anna took one off the rack and glanced at the headline about some fresh Royal scandal with a grimace. It seemed that the papers had all been full of the same story lately—although this was probably a few days out of date now.

Her eyes found the date printed at the top as she slotted the paper back into the rack and she felt the shock spear through her so fast that she gasped out loud. For a moment she couldn't move; the numbers were glaring back at her yet they made absolutely no sense!

She took a long, slow breath, her heart pounding

as she made herself focus on the date once more, but it was still the same, unchanged. It was only she who was different, her whole world which had been suddenly turned upside down, because it seemed that the date was one whole year later than she had thought it to be!

'Signora Falcone? Are you all right?'

Anna responded instinctively, turning to look at the shopkeeper, seeing the concern on his face. It didn't seem to matter all that much. What did matter was the fact that twelve whole months of her life were missing. The world had moved on and she had lived that year, but it was a blank, like a sheet of paper with nothing written on it.

'*Signora*, please, come inside while I telephone your husband.' The man urged her towards the door and Anna experienced the ridiculous urge to laugh. Telephone Riccardo on a phone which didn't work because of a storm which hadn't happened? Telephone her husband on a day twelve months on from what she had thought it to be... But did Riccardo know that there was this huge gap in her memory?

She closed her eyes and felt herself go cold as she instantly recalled that conversation she'd had with Patrick Grady about how long she had been married, Riccardo's cool confirmation of her mistake minutes later...!

'I send for the *dottore*, *si*? Please come inside, *signora*.'

She roused herself with an effort as the man tried to lead her into the shop. She'd had enough of doctors and people telling her things supposedly for her own good. What she needed now was time to think, time to work out why Riccardo had lied to her! 'No, thank you. I'm fine. Really.'

She hurried back along the street, turning down the first opening she came to with no idea where she was heading. Yet when she found herself down by the river it seemed that maybe her unconscious had led her there, to the place where it had all begun. Would she find here the answers she so desperately needed? How could there be any answer to why Riccardo had deceived her?

She lay down on the cool grass, suddenly overcome by exhaustion and slowly, inch by inch, the door to her mind opened just that little bit more. . .

'I shall be late this evening. Do not wait dinner for me, Anna. I shall have something brought in to the office.'

'Again? But, Ricco, that is the third time this week. Surely you can make an effort to be home for once?'

Her voice sounded petulant even to her, and she bit her lip. She had been feeling unwell for the past few days, vague feelings of nausea combined with an unexpected lethargy which had left her with little energy. But that wasn't any excuse for sounding like a peevish wife when she knew that Riccardo wouldn't have stayed at the office unless it was for something urgent!

When he came to kiss her, his handsome face slightly set, she put her arms around his neck and pulled him down to her, pressing her mouth to his in a kiss far warmer than the cool token he'd intended. 'I'm sorry, Ricco. I sound like a horrible nagging wife, don't I?'

'*Si.*' He laughed suddenly, his eyes crinkling at the corners, his mouth curled into a devastatingly attractive smile. 'But I still love you, *cara*, despite your desire to play the shrew!'

'Rat!' She nipped his lower lip in loving punishment and felt the surge his body gave as he drew her up from the chair and held her against him. His kiss was as thorough as she could have wished it to be—no token this time, but full of the passion they had shared each and every day of their lives until lately, when Riccardo had been so distracted with work.

Anna drew back, staring up at him with eyes soft with love. 'Can't you tell me what is bothering you, darling? It's obvious that something is wrong.'

He sighed heavily before he made an obvious effort to smile. 'It is just some irritating problem which I shall solve eventually.' He smoothed a kiss across her temple, brushing the silky hair aside so that his lips could trace the delicate blue veins which throbbed beneath her fine skin. 'It is nothing to worry about, Anna. Once I have it under control then I think we shall take a little holiday, perhaps go to England to visit your friends—even the dreaded Nell.'

Anna laughed. 'Riccardo! How can you? Nell is my best friend and I love her dearly. We've known each other for years, so that she is almost family to me. But, yes, darling I would love to do that—

although perhaps we could leave the visiting until the end of our trip. I would much prefer to spend the time alone with you.'

He kissed her hard and passionately, his eyes making silent promises. 'Then that is what we shall do, *cara.*' He framed her face between his hands, his face suddenly very grave. 'You love me, do you not, Anna? You love me enough to believe in me, to understand that sometimes other people are unable to see the truth that you see with your heart?'

She couldn't understand what he meant, yet suddenly felt afraid. 'You know I do, Ricco! What is it? Has something happened?'

He nodded, his thumbs smoothing her soft cheeks. '*Si.* But I shall work it out. Knowing that you believe in me is enough to help me through this difficult time.'

He gave her one last swift kiss, then left before Anna could ask him anything more. She sat down at the table, feeling deeply disturbed. She knew that this problem Riccardo was dealing with must be something major, but had no idea what it was. Her mind raced back and forth as she tried to work it out, but it was impossible. For now all she could do was be there for him to offer support. She smiled tenderly—where else would she want to be?

She worked late that day, in the huge, airy studio Riccardo had had built for her as a surprise when they got back from their honeymoon. The painting had been going well, but today Anna found that her concentration kept lapsing. She couldn't stop wondering how Riccardo was. Suddenly impatient to know, she left the studio and hurried downstairs to the study to phone him, but just as she got there the telephone rang.

Startled, Anna pressed a hand to her jumping heart, laughing when she recognised Riccardo's deep voice. 'Darling, I was just about to ring you! We must be—'

'Anna, I want you to listen carefully to what I tell you to do.' He cut her off, his voice so unlike its usual tone that she felt suddenly cold.

'What's wrong? Riccardo, tell me what has happened!' Her fingers ached from the pressure as she clasped the telephone, suddenly afraid.

'I have no time to explain. You must just do as I ask.' He sounded furiously angry. Anna could almost feel the anger rippling along the line, and it scared her more than ever.

'Open the top drawer of my desk and there you will find a small notebook with names and telephone numbers in it. I want you to look for the number of Eduardo Rossi, then telephone him and tell him that I need him to come to the *commisariato* immediately. Do you understand?'

'Yes! No! I don't understand any of it. Ricco, what's going on? Why are you with the police? Has there been an accident?' The fear was making her feel sick. Anna fought against it, refusing to give in when it seemed Riccardo needed her help so desperately.

'There has been no accident! This has been no act of God but of man, *cara*. Now do as I tell you.'

He had hung up before Anna could say anything

more. For a moment she stared at the phone, then dropped the receiver. What was going on? Why was Riccardo at the police station? Who was this Eduardo Rossi he wanted her to call?

She wrenched the desk drawer open and found the notebook lying on the top of a pile of papers and files. She thumbed through it, then dialled the number with shaking hands, stumbling into halting Italian when a man answered, and was overwhelmed with relief when he responded in perfect English.

'Oh, thank heavens. I need to speak to Eduardo Rossi urgently.'

'This is Rossi. How may I help you, *signora*?'

The voice sounded middle-aged, calm and cultured, and did a lot to steady her. 'I am ringing for my husband, Riccardo Falcone. He has just telephoned me, *signore*, and asked me to tell you that he needs you to go to the police station immediately.' She took a quick gasping breath, her heart hammering. 'I don't know why; he didn't say. He just sounded as though it was imperative you get there right away.'

'Then rest assured I shall not let him down, Signora Falcone. I shall leave immediately.'

'But what is it about? Do you have any idea?' She could hear her voice echoing with confusion and fear.

Eduardo Rossi seemed to hesitate, then said smoothly, 'I am sure that it is nothing Riccardo and I cannot sort out. Leave it to me, *signora*, and do not distress yourself too much.'

Anna replaced the receiver and sat staring across

the room. How could she not worry? What was going on? She went to slip the notebook back into the drawer then stopped, her eyes drawn to the corner of a photograph sticking out from one of the files. Riccardo had albums full of photographs which she had looked at many times—studying the strong resemblance he bore to his dead father, Alessandro, observing the way his mother had obviously doted on him. So what was this picture doing here in the drawer?

Driven by a sudden curiosity, she pulled it out. . .

'Anna! *Cara*, speak to me!'

Riccardo's hand stroking her hair. Riccardo's voice pulling her back from the past. Anna opened her eyes, staring up at him with shock. 'You were at the police station. . .! You telephoned me and told me to call someone called Eduardo Rossi.'

His face tightened, his eyes burning like silver flames, his whole body rigid with sudden tension. 'You have remembered, Anna? Is that what has happened?'

She shook her head, striving to hang onto the memories which were dissolving like mist. 'I. . . I don't know,' she whispered. 'I remember some of it, but not all. Yet I don't understand any of it, Ricco!'

She tried to sit up, then gasped when he swept her up in his arms and carried her up the bank to where his car was parked, the door hanging open as though he hadn't taken time to close it. When Riccardo eased her gently down into the seat Anna let her head drop back against the soft leather, too drained even to look at him.

He leant across and turned her face towards him, his silver eyes burning. 'When they came from the town and told me what had happened and I couldn't find you I was so afraid, Anna! So desperately afraid.'

'I'm afraid too, Riccardo.' Her eyes met his, the pain shadowing their depths as she searched his face. 'I thought I knew you but I was wrong, so very wrong. You're a stranger, Riccardo. I don't know how you think or feel any longer.' She gave a broken laugh, seeing the flicker of emotion which crossed his face. 'Perhaps I never really did know you—just thought that I did!'

'Anna, you are overwrought. This has been too much for you. . .'

'Yes, I am overwrought! And who can blame me? Which woman wouldn't feel as I do discovering that the man she loves, her husband, has lied to her? You knew that a year of my memory was missing but you never told me. Why, Riccardo?'

She gave a bitter little laugh as she saw the shock cross his face. 'Yes, I discovered it when I looked at one of the English newspapers in the town. It suddenly hit me that twelve months were missing. You have to be incredibly arrogant to have believed that you could get away with it—but then, isn't that what you are? Riccardo Falcone can do and act however he likes, and to hell with everyone! To hell with me, in fact!'

'No! It was not like that. I promise you, Anna,

that everything I have ever done has been out of love for you. Can you not find it in your heart to believe that?'

He took her hand and held it tightly, his eyes burning into hers. He seemed to be willing her to believe him, and once she would have done so—because believing in Riccardo had made everything right. Her love for him had coloured her whole world. . .and blinded her to the truth. It was the bitterest pain imaginable to face it.

'I doubt I can ever again believe anything you tell me, Riccardo. I don't know why you did what you did. I assume you had a reason for keeping me in the dark about something so important, but I don't think I shall ever forgive you for the way you have deceived me.' She drew her hand away and turned to stare out of the window with empty eyes and a heart which was even emptier.

'I did what I felt necessary, Anna. I hoped that you would understand that everything I have ever done has been for your own good.'

His deep voice held a note of condemnation which brought tears to her eyes as she looked at him. 'Maybe if you had told me more then I would have understood. Do you know what I have discovered in the past week or so since we got here, Ricco? Just how little I really know about you.

'If someone came to me and said, Tell me about your husband—what kind of man he really is, how he thinks, what he believes in, I would be hard pressed to do so. We might have been married for two years, not one, but I have come to realise that I know less about you than I might know about a stranger!'

He started the engine, his hands gripping the wheel tightly for a moment as he looked at her. 'I love you, Anna. Once that would have been all you needed to know. Now it seems it isn't enough.'

Wasn't it? She turned away, sitting unmoving as Riccardo drove the car away from the river. Once the thought that Riccardo loved her had filled her whole world; now that same world seemed to be crumbling around her. She heard the words but was no longer sure what they meant or what to believe. And if she lost her ability to believe in Riccardo then she would lose everything.

CHAPTER SEVEN

THE drive back to the Villa Margherita was over too quickly. Anna wished that it could have gone on and on, because while they were driving she could put off the moment of confrontation that bit longer, but all too soon, it seemed, Riccardo turned into the driveway and drew the car to a careful halt.

He turned to look at her, but Anna made no attempt to return his gaze as she opened the car door and climbed out. Without a backward glance she went indoors, hearing Riccardo's footsteps following as she crossed the hall. But when she went to start up the stairs he stopped her.

'No. What has happened needs discussing, Anna.'

'Discussing? Don't you mean that you will think up some more lies to stop me asking questions you don't want to answer for some unknown reason?' She couldn't keep the sarcasm from her voice, couldn't hold back the anguish she felt as she turned to look at him at last. She loved him so much but he couldn't love her—not when he had lied to her, deceived her. . .

'I have never lied to you!' His voice reflected his anger, his face hard and set as he stared at her.

Anna met his gaze, a fierce pride determining that she did not break down. 'No? Then obviously your view of the truth differs greatly from mine, Riccardo!

You knew very well that I thought it was last year, and that somehow I must have forgotten everything that has happened since then, but you made no attempt to help me remember, did you?'

She gave a bitter laugh. 'No wonder Patrick Grady was confused! There he was, telling me that he thought we had been married for two years, and there was I, assuring him that he was wrong with you backing me up! Why, Riccardo? That's all I want to know—although I don't suppose there is much point in even asking that, because I doubt if I would believe what you told me now!'

She swung round to run up the stairs, almost blinded by tears, then gasped when Riccardo unceremoniously hauled her back round. His hands clamped on the fragile bones of her shoulders, his eyes burning as he stared into her shocked face.

'Do not ever speak to me that way! Do you hear me, Anna? You have gone too far this time!'

'I. . .' She didn't know what to do. She stood there staring up into the face of the man who was her husband and saw there a stranger! Fear ran through her and she started to struggle, beating at his chest and shoulders with her clenched fists until he swore roughly—words she couldn't understand but whose meaning was more than clear as he swung her off her feet and strode up the stairs with her struggling in his arms.

He kicked the bedroom door open, then strode across the room and dropped her onto the bed, his chest heaving as he glared down at her. 'You asked me why I didn't tell you that you had forgotten a year of your life and I shall tell you, *cara*. Even though, you said so clearly, you will not believe me.'

'I don't want to hear anything you have to tell me!' Anna scrambled across the huge bed, her legs tangling in the flowing skirts of her dress so that Riccardo had no difficulty in stopping her. He pushed her back against the soft pillows and held her there with one large hand.

'Perhaps you do not, *innamorata*, but I wish to tell you, and you will stay there and listen.' His silver eyes blazed, his mouth was a thin tight line, and a rim of colour burned along his cheekbones.

Anna felt the jolt of shock ripple through her as she realised that Riccardo was within a hair's breadth of losing control. She had never seen him this way before, had never looked into his face and seen that wildness there, and it frightened her even more. She started to struggle again, but with his hand holding her down she had no choice but to stay where she was, and she heard him laugh softly.

'*Si, cara mia.* You realise that I mean what I say.' He sat down beside her, bending to look straight into her huge green eyes. Anna took a shuddery little breath and turned her head away, but Riccardo turned it back and held it there. 'I did not set out to deliberately deceive you, Anna. Oh, I realised from small things you said in the hospital that there was something wrong, but until we were driving here from the airport I did not understand how much of your memory was missing.'

Anna could feel the thunderous pounding of her

heart in every cell, the hard pressure of Riccardo's hand against her chest, the lighter touch of his fingers against her jaw, and felt at that moment as though she was trapped—trapped by Riccardo, trapped by her own inability to remember, trapped by whatever was waiting to emerge from the past to hurt her! And fear gave her the courage to speak her mind.

'Then why didn't you say something? Maybe not then, but later? I cannot believe that there wasn't a single opportunity to tell me the truth!'

'Maybe you are right. Maybe I should have told you, Anna, but I did not.' He laughed bitterly, his handsome face like a mask. 'I suppose I imagined that you would trust me to do what I thought best, that when you finally remembered you would accept that I had. But now I can see I was wrong to make such an assumption. Perhaps it was expecting too much that you simply trust me, your husband.'

That was so unfair! Anna's eyes blazed back at him, her face tinged with soft colour, her breasts rising and falling beneath the soft cotton bodice of her dress. 'Don't off-load your own guilt on me, Riccardo! It would have been simple enough to tell me that I had made a mistake after Patrick Grady had been here. You could have explained that a year was missing, but instead you chose to carry on with the charade. Why? You must have had a reason, presumably, so what was it? I think I have a right to know why you took such a decision upon yourself, don't you?'

His hands gripped her so hard that she winced,

yet he appeared not to notice. 'Because I was afraid! Can you not understand that? I was afraid, Anna!'

Her breath caught with shock, so that suddenly she was unaware of the painful grip of his fingers. 'Afraid? Of what? Tell me, Ricco!'

He let her go abruptly and got up, walking across the room to stop with his back towards her. He ran a hand over his hair and around the back of his neck, and Anna was shocked to see how it trembled.

'Ricco. . .'

He turned around, his face partly shadowed but his eyes glittering with an emotion which made her feel raw and shaken just to witness it. 'Of losing you! I do not think I could bear that, *cara*—do not think I would want to live in a world where you no longer wanted me.' He held his hand up when she started to speak, although what she was going to say, Anna had no idea. Why should he ever think that he would lose her?

She felt a cold shiver run through her. An echo from the past or a premonition for the future? That was the trouble; she had no idea which because there was this huge blank in her mind—a massive piece missing from the puzzle, not just the tiny bits she'd once imagined.

'No. Let me speak. It is time I did so—way past the time, in fact—but I was too much of a coward to do so before and take the risk.' His hands clenched into fists but Anna could see nothing on his face, no emotion at all, and with a sudden flash of painful insight she realised that for Riccardo to show any at that moment would have been too much.

'I should have told you the truth as soon as it became apparent that you did not remember, but that year you have forgotten was not a year I wished to remember either. So many things went wrong in those months, Anna. So many things happened which threatened our love, then suddenly they were all gone from your mind. It was as though we had been given a second chance at happiness and I was greedy and desperate enough to snatch it.'

He shrugged. 'Perhaps it was wrong, but with the doctors insisting that you allow your memory to return of its own accord, I saw it as a blessing. I hoped, prayed, that if we just had enough time then you would fall in love with me again and that when your memory returned we would have that to bind us together. But I can see now that I was wrong to make such a decision.'

Anna's eyes swam with tears, the soft confession affecting her as no amount of harsh words could have done. Riccardo was so proud and self-assured, a man who lived his life by his own rigorous standards, yet he had laid his soul bare to her just now by admitting his innermost fears.

She knelt up on the bed, her need to reassure him of her love of paramount importance so that what he had done seemed to pale into insignificance. How could Riccardo have believed even for a moment that she had stopped loving him?

'I do love you, Riccardo. Nothing can ever change that. Loving you is the single most important thing in my life. I don't know what went wrong that year, but whatever it was I can't believe it was anything which would stop me from loving you!'

He came back to the bed, staring down at her for a long moment before he sat beside her and took her hands in his. 'Love is a precious gift, Anna. Once I did not believe it even existed, but then I met you. It is hard to imagine that once given love can be taken back, but things happen. . .things which can alter how one feels.'

She gave a shaky little laugh which reflected her unease. 'So what did happen to make you believe I might have stopped loving you?'

He seemed to hesitate, then lifted her hands to his mouth and kissed them gently. 'How much do you remember?'

Anna shrugged, feeling the sudden stir of her senses as his cool mouth touched her skin. 'Just bits—odd, disjointed things which don't make much sense. The fact that you had some problem you were dealing with. . .a telephone call you made one night, asking me to contact someone called Eduardo Rossi. . .' She searched her mind, wondering why she had the feeling that there was something else, but it escaped her. She sighed. 'That's about it. I. . . I still can't remember the baby, though.'

'In time you will. In time it will all become clear again, when your mind is strong enough to accept it. But what you have just spoken of all happened and put a strain on our happiness.'

'But why?'

'Because I ended up working far too hard in my business and I think you felt neglected. You had come to live in a strange country, and that was hard enough, but to have me absent all the time. . . And then, after you lost the baby, we did not seem able to talk as we once had. We grew apart.' He shrugged, but there was an intentness to the look he gave her.

Anna looked away, letting what he had told her sink deeper into her mind, wishing that she could remember. She could understand that her grief over the loss of their child must have affected her badly, but was she the sort of woman who needed constant attention lavished on her? She didn't think so.

After her parents had been killed in that tragic car crash when she was ten, her grandmother had cared for her. Helen Becket had been in her late sixties by then, and unable to do the things with her granddaughter that a younger woman would have done. Anna had grown used to filling the time with her own pursuits, so that being on her own had never been a problem.

And yet as one part of her mind started to deny what Riccardo had said the other recalled with sudden clarity that conversation she'd remembered, with her voice sounding so petulant as she'd nagged Riccardo about not being home for dinner again.

'You were caught up with some problem,' she said tentatively. 'Was that what was keeping you away so much?'

He smiled at her, his eyes warm as they traced her face. '*Si.* It was not out of choice, *cara mia.* If the choice had been mine then I would have simply delegated my responsibilities and spent more time with you, which was what I wanted to do. But unfortunately I was the only one who could deal with what was happening.'

'How did it involve Eduardo Rossi? Who is he, Ricco?' She gave him a small smile, feeling some of the warmth flowing back into her. Everything Riccardo had told her made sense, even though she might not agree with his decision to protect her the way he had. He must have been driven to do so, yet the idea of her ever stopping loving him was ridiculous! Nothing could ever change how she felt about him.

Something of her feelings must have shown, because he bent and kissed her hard, his eyes blazing. 'I adore you, *cara*. Always remember that.'

He drew back, smoothing the backs of her hands with his thumbs in gentle strokes which lit fires inside her. 'Eduardo Rossi is an old friend and my lawyer. There had been attempts made to discredit my business, and that day I asked you to contact him things had come to a head. The police had "invited" me down to speak to them about several matters which had arisen, and I deemed it necessary to have Eduardo there.'

'Discredit your business. . .what do you mean?' Anna frowned in consternation.

'Rumours circulating, orders cancelled apparently by my office, when in fact we had not done so—things like that. Then that week there were problems with one of my shipments.' Richards sighed. 'My firm came under the scrutiny of the authorities, but with Eduardo's help I was able to convince them that I had no knowledge of what had happened. But at the time it was very worrying. My reputation was at stake, you understand?'

'But that's dreadful! And you really believe that someone had deliberately set out to damage your business? But who?'

He gave a harsh laugh which held a wealth of experience.

'I imagine there are many who would be pleased to witness my downfall!'

Anna shuddered A man in Riccardo's position would always arouse jealousy in others less fortunate, but he sounded almost as though he expected it. How could he be so calm when she found the idea both scary and distasteful? 'It is all sorted out now, though, isn't it? Why, only the other day you mentioned that there was a problem you were having to deal with. . .?'

'Everything is in hand, Anna. There is no need to worry yourself.'

'So it isn't resolved yet,' she guessed, sickened by the thought of Riccardo being a target for some unknown person's spite. 'That is why you asked Patrick Grady to help you?'

'*Si.* You are very astute, my love. Whilst the police have accepted that I was not at fault they have not discovered who was behind it, and I would like to know.'

'But who is Patrick Grady? Some sort of private detective?'

Riccardo laughed. 'In a way. He runs a news

agency which specialises in stories which prove difficult to get to the bottom of, and as such he has many contacts which should prove beneficial now. But let us not talk any more about such matters when there is no need, Anna. Leave me to deal with them.'

He drew her to him, his arms sliding around her as he held her close and kissed her forehead. I shall never forgive myself for what happened today. That you should have been so distressed because of my foolishness. . .'

Anna slid her arms around his waist and nestled closer, drawing comfort from the feel of his hard body although it was impossible simply to dismiss the thought of someone deliberately trying to hurt Riccardo. 'You did it because you love me, Ricco.'

He tilted her face to look deep into her eyes. 'You understand that now? You believe that I would never do anything to harm you?'

'Of course!' She laughed softly, feeling the first flames of desire licking through her body, welcoming them again. It seemed so long since she had felt their warmth, too long since she had been able to set aside her fears and uncertainties, but now she could. Riccardo had been fighting for her love, or so he'd thought—because nothing could ever take that away from him. But his vulnerability touched her deeply, making her love him even more because of it!

When he bent and kissed her Anna responded with all the passion she could feel inside her, and heard the deep groan he gave. He drew back, a tiny nerve beating in his jaw, desire burning in his eyes.

'We should not do this, *cara*. We must remember what the doctor said, and today you have been upset...'

She ran her hands up his chest, feeling the warm, hard muscles beneath his silk shirt, the faint rasp of body hair. His heart was beating so hard that it shook him, and her own heart reflected its rapid pounding. 'Sometimes doctors don't know everything, Riccardo. Sometimes it is far, far better to rely on instinct.'

Her voice was a husky invitation, her green eyes full of promises as they held his, and she felt him tense. Riccardo was fighting to be sensible—a battle that she was determined he was going to lose!

Anna brushed her mouth across his, letting her lips linger softly against the beautiful chiselled hardness of his, and heard the low, self-mocking laugh he gave at his own weakness as he suddenly pulled her hard against him.

'Witch! You cast your spell over me and make it so hard to be sensible. I have been enticed by your beauty ever since we first met, and that will never change!'

His mouth was suddenly urgent, demanding, his hands moving to the tiny buttons down the bodice of her dress as he gently pressed her back against the pillows. Anna ran her fingers through his dark hair, watching his face as he slowly opened them. She hadn't worn a bra because the weather was far too hot for such a restriction, and as Riccardo pushed the soft folds of cotton aside her small firm breasts were suddenly bare to his gaze.

'Exquisite.' Then he lapsed into mellifluous Italian, his hands tracing the soft curves of her body, his lips following them as he reverently kissed each breast, teasing and arousing until Anna writhed beneath his tormenting hands, wanting only the satisfaction he could give her.

'I love you!'

Her voice rang around the room as finally they joined together and reconfirmed their love for one another, and Riccardo's echoed it. Anna clung to him as the hot flames of passion slowly died to a languid heat, and smiled in sweet contentment, more at peace than she had felt for days.

Sunlight was streaming through the open shutters, a great swathe of golden light catching their two bodies in its path, almost as though heaven was smiling down on them. It seemed like an omen for the future, a reassurance that all the darkness had fled. Now, with Riccardo in her arms and her love for him in her heart, she had no fears, and gradually she drifted off to sleep.

Yet just as she was between sleep and wakefulness she remembered that photograph she had seen in the drawer that night... But it couldn't hold any significance now that Riccardo had explained away her fears.

'You are enjoying yourself, *cara*?

'Of course! It was a lovely idea to come out for the evening—a sort of celebration.'

Riccardo understood at once because his face softened. He raised his glass and touched it to hers. 'A celebration, indeed, Anna. To us and our love.'

Anna raised her own glass and sipped the wine, then smiled at Riccardo as she set it down. She had been thrilled when he had suddenly announced that they would go out to dinner that evening, and it had been everything she could have wished for.

Being with Riccardo like this was healing after all the traumas they had both suffered. She had been plagued with so many doubts, but he had had his own fears to deal with—although nothing in the whole wide world could ever change how she felt about him!

There was a small band playing soft, romantic tunes inside the restaurant, and the music flowed out onto the terrace where they had chosen to dine. When Riccardo got up and held his hand out to her, Anna placed hers into it and let him lead her onto the grass beneath the tall cypress trees. He drew her gently into his arms, his hands warm as they pressed against the small of her back while they moved slowly to the pulsing rhythm of the music. Several other couples were dancing as well, but Anna felt as though she and Riccardo were the only two people in the world just then. . .

'*Che sorpresa*! I never expected to see you two here.'

The woman's voice sent a cold jolt of recognition through Anna at once. She turned towards the elegant brunette with her heart sinking. She had met her socially on several occasions but had never liked her, aware each time they'd met of the other woman's animosity towards her. Now, as Riccardo drew her to a halt, Anna steeled herself for this unwelcome meeting.

'Sofia. I did not realise that you had discovered this place.'

Sofia gave a tinkly little laugh, her dark eyes flashing at the cool note in Riccardo's voice. 'Did you not, *caro*? Perhaps that is the reason why you chose to come here, so that you could avoid your friends?'

Riccardo stared back at her, his silver eyes cold, his mouth thinned with displeasure. 'I am always pleased to see *friends*, Sofia.'

Sofia flushed and turned to Anna, her dark eyes holding such loathing that instinctively Anna stiffened. 'How are you, Anna? It is a long time since we saw each other, is it not? And how you have changed.'

Sofia's eyes went to her hair, and for the first time Anna felt self-conscious of her appearance. Her hand lifted before she managed to stop it, and she knew from the glitter of amusement in Sofia's eyes that the woman had noticed the betraying gesture.

Anna drew herself up, determined not to let Sofia think that she had got the better of her. 'I'm sure I have. But you haven't changed, Sofia. You are just the same as you always were.'

There was no need for her to say anything more as they both understood. Sofia's red mouth compressed, the look she gave her enough to cut her to shreds, but Anna ignored it as she turned to

Riccardo. 'Excuse me, darling, I'll just go and freshen up.'

'Of course.' Riccardo kissed her hand, his eyes following her as she made her way back inside the restaurant.

Anna hurried into the rest-room and stared into the mirror, seeing the over-bright glitter of her eyes, the stark pallor of her skin—outward evidence of the unpleasantness of that brief exchange.

Riccardo had told her that he and Sofia had once had an affair, although he hadn't needed to because she had remembered the woman the first time she had seen her again at a dinner party one night. Sofia had been with Riccardo that day they had met down by the river, and Anna knew that the other woman's animosity stemmed from that. She had taken Riccardo away from Sofia and the woman hated her because of it, but surely Sofia could see that the relationship had been doomed to failure if it hadn't survived even a chance meeting?

The sudden opening of the door made her jump. Anna looked up and felt her heart sink as she saw through the mirror Sofia coming into the room. Hurriedly she picked up her bag, wanting to avoid any further unpleasantness, but evidently Sofia wasn't prepared to let her get away that easily.

She stepped in front of Anna, smiling as she studied her from top to toe. 'I never could understand what Riccardo saw in you, Anna, and now less than ever. What have you been doing with yourself whilst you have been away?'

Anna coloured, feeling her anger stirring to life.

'I am sure you wouldn't really be interested, Sofia. Now, if you will excuse me. . .'

'Oh, but not so quickly.' She gave a harsh little laugh as she took a step closer, so that Anna was forced to back up against the washbasins. 'Surely we should take time to renew our acquaintance? And it is only natural that I should be interested, as all Riccardo's friends will be when they discover that you have turned up again. . .how do you say?. . . ahh, yes. . .like the bad pennies?'

'I have no idea what you are talking about. Please let me pass.' Anna clutched her bag, her hands trembling. She didn't want to hear another word Sofia had to say, didn't want anything to spoil this wonderful evening.

'Come, Anna, you cannot brush aside the fact that you walked out on Riccardo almost a year ago. Frankly, I cannot understand why he would have you back after the way you behaved, but. . .'

Sofia shrugged as she glanced into the mirror to brush a loose strand of her hair back into place, missing Anna's shocked gasp.

'Walked out on Riccardo. . .! What do you mean?'

Sofia started, the shrillness of Anna's voice obviously getting through to her. 'You know what I mean. Why pretend? Do you hope that people will simply forget what you did? Oh, Riccardo refused to discuss it, of course. I am sure he was simply too angry to speak about what you had done. But that he should have taken you back seems beyond belief.'

Sofia laughed—an ugly sound which held a wealth

of venom. 'Unless he has something planned, of course—some way to make you pay for the insult you gave him. To walk out on Riccardo Falcone of all people must be the ultimate foolishness, but to dare to come back to him seems like absolute madness. Yes, Anna, I am sure that Riccardo has some reason for taking you back into his life!

Sofia spun round on her elegant high heels and calmly left the room. Anna stood where she was, wondering if she was going to be sick. Could Sofia have been telling the truth or had she been lying? She didn't know because she couldn't remember... she simply couldn't remember! Her heart lurched as realisation struck her. Sofia didn't know that, though. Sofia knew nothing about the accident and its after-effects, so why would she risk telling such a lie? ,

'Anna. . .*cara*, are you all right?'

Riccardo's voice came through the closed door and Anna jumped violently. She stared at the door with wild eyes, every word Sofia had said echoing inside her head. Was it possible that it had been the truth—that she had left Riccardo? But how—why? And where had she been since?

'Anna, answer me!'

Riccardo's voice grated with concern, and Anna took a quick little breath and forced herself to speak, although her voice sounded as hollow and empty as she felt. Had Sofia also been speaking the truth about why Riccardo had taken her back? Had he done so not because he loved her but because he wanted her to pay for what she had done? The thought made her feel ill!

'I. . . I won't be long.'

'You are all right?'

He still sounded concerned, and Anna closed her eyes on a wave of pain, realising that she could no longer believe anything any more. 'Yes,' she whispered. 'Yes, I'm fine.'

'I shall wait for you on the terrace, then.'

She heard his footsteps retreating and slumped over the basin as sickness claimed her. Rinsing her face in cold water, she stared at her reflection and tried to force the mist from her mind, but it was impossible. She had no idea what the truth was—if Sofia had been lying or not. Nothing made sense any more, but suddenly she knew that for both her sake and Riccardo's she had to know what had happened. . .all of it!

CHAPTER EIGHT

'I HOPE meeting Sofia did not upset you, *cara*. She will regret speaking like that to you, believe me!'

Anna started, shooting a wary glance at Riccardo. They had spoken little so far on the drive back from the restaurant. Anna had been too caught up with her own thoughts and Riccardo had seemed to be concentrating on negotiating the twisting roads, yet obviously his mind wasn't solely on that task.

When he turned to glance at her she looked away, afraid of what he might see on her face right then—all the anguish and confusion. Had Sofia been lying or not? She should by rights simply ask Riccardo, but she was scared to do that in case the answer was one she wouldn't want to hear!

'I am to blame, of course, Anna. I see that now, when it is too late to change things.'

'What do you mean?' Her voice was no more than a husky murmur, her face very pale in the dim light from the dashboard. When Riccardo muttered something and touched her hand she jumped visibly.

He drew the car to a stop at the side of the road and switched on the interior light. 'You are upset, and that is the last thing I wanted to happen, *cara mia*. If I had guessed that Sofia might be there tonight...' He shrugged, his meaning more than clear, but the reasons behind it not nearly so. Was

Riccardo sorry that they had met Sofia because of the unpleasantness, or worried about what she might have said?

Anna's hands clenched, her heart pounding. 'Sofia has never liked me. I think she believes that I took you away from her.'

'*Si.* And she is right. When I met you, Anna, I could think of no other woman. I was, perhaps, unnecessarily harsh with Sofia, and now I regret that. But she always knew there were limits to our relationship.'

'In what way were you hard on Sofia?'

He sighed heavily, leaning back in the seat, his expression one of intense weariness. Anna experienced the deepest urge to reach out and touch him, to close her mind to these new fears. But how could she? Of all the uncertainties which had gone before these seemed the worst.

'Do you remember that night I saw you in the café in the piazza? It was just a few hours after we had met.'

She nodded. 'Yes, I remember it well. It was one of the first things I did remember in the hospital, in fact.'

He glanced at her with a gentle smile. 'I, too, was thinking about it then, Anna. Our thoughts must have been in harmony—but then we always did share so much, right from the beginning. You knew how I felt when we met because you felt it too, even though neither of us really understood what was happening.'

He gave a soft laugh, reaching out to brush her

cheek with his knuckles. 'I was fired by such urgency to see you again, and impatient with anything which got in my way. Sofia and some friends were staying at the villa at that time, and somehow she must have guessed where I was going that night. She was angry, but so was I, and I spoke to her far more abruptly than I should have done—told her that I did not care if she was still there when I got back.' He paused. 'I regret not that I told her the truth but that I did it in such a way. I suspect that is the cause of her hostility towards you.'

It would be so easy to accept that as the explanation. Sofia hated her because her pride had been hurt, and that was why she had thought up that tale. But would Sofia risk telling a lie like that? Not unless. . .unless Sofia had found out about her loss of memory and was playing upon the fact that Anna wouldn't be able to disprove what she said! Sofia must be well aware that Riccardo would deny her accusations if he was guilty and deny them just as vehemently if he wasn't, so that the doubts would always be left in Anna's mind!

Hope rose so swiftly that Anna could barely speak. 'Does. . .does Sofia know about my stay in hospital?'

If Riccardo found anything odd in the question he gave no sign as he started the engine again. 'No.'

'Are you sure? Someone might have mentioned it to her—another friend of you both, perhaps?'

Riccardo shot her a quick glance, obviously hearing the urgency in her tone. 'I have mentioned nothing about your illness to anyone. Why are you asking me this, Anna? Did Sofia say something to make you think she knew about the accident?'

On the contrary! Anna bit her lip as the brief, bright hope flickered and died. 'No. I... I just wondered, that's all.'

She closed her eyes as Riccardo drew the car back onto the road, feigning sleep to stop any further conversation. She had never felt so desolate in all her life. How would she bear it if she found out that Sofia had been telling the truth?

The moon was a silver ball in the velvet sky when they drew up in front of the villa. Riccardo came around to help Anna from the car but she pretended not to see his outstretched hand as she hurriedly got out. She started towards the house faster than she ought to have done on the rough gravel, then cried out when her heel caught in the stones and pitched her forwards.

Riccardo had her in his arms in a trice, holding her close as he steadied her. 'Careful, my darling. You are tired, I think. I was going to suggest that we have a nightcap, but perhaps it would be better if you went straight up to bed.'

Anna nodded, afraid to say anything in case she broke down. Feeling Riccardo so close was the bitterest kind of torment when they had never seemed so far apart before.

She went up to their room and stood for a long while, trying to make sense of everything she had learned tonight, but it was impossible. Sofia had either lied or she hadn't, and her whole future hinged on finding out which it was. And it seemed the only way she might do that was by going to Milan.

With a heavy heart, Anna showered and changed into a cool white cotton nightgown, then switched off the lamp and climbed into the big old bed. But sleep proved impossible. She was still awake when Riccardo came upstairs some while later, opening the door quietly so as not to disturb her. He had taken off his jacket and unbuttoned the collar of his shirt, but he didn't look relaxed as he stood in the doorway for a moment.

Anna watched him from under her lashes, seeing the tension in him as he finally closed the door. It seemed that Riccardo had something on his mind, and her heart sank at the thought of what it mght be. He hung his jacket up, then turned to go to the bathroom, and must have sensed her watching him. He came over to the bed, his face all dark shadows in the pale moonlight spilling through the open window, his silver eyes translucent.

'Can you not sleep?'

Anna shook her head, her voice just as soft as Riccardo's had been. 'No. My mind is too busy.'

He sighed with a wealth of wearines as he sat down beside her and lifted her hand from where it lay on the lace coverlet. 'I wish that we could shut out the world, Anna, then I am sure we would both be happy.'

'Would we?' Her fingers twined between his, feeling the strength in his grip. She wished that she could draw on that strength now, as she had done in the past. 'Is it just the outside world which is making life so difficult, or is it something we have brought upon ourselves?'

His gaze was suddenly fierce. 'Perhaps it is a bit of both. But we need not let the world intrude if we do not choose to. Here in this special place there is just you and me and what we mean to one another. Nothing else matters, *cara*, nothing!'

His mouth was urgent as it claimed hers, fiercely possessive, as though he was determined to convince her that what he said was right. Anna felt her senses flare at once, felt desire run through her like a hot flame which melted away the cold edges of uncertainty. When Riccardo kissed her this way she could almost believe that only this mattered, what they felt here and now in each other's arms! Was this the answer she was seeking—the absolute truth?

'Anna. . . Anna!'

He lapsed into soft Italian, his deep voice husky with emotions before he drew back just a fraction, to stare down at her almost as though he wanted to say something. Anna could see the fire in his silver eyes, the desire in the taut set of his jaw, and knew that words were unnecessary. When Riccardo looked at her this way she could believe in him and his love totally!

'No. Don't say anything.' She pressed her fingers to his hard mouth, her own eyes blazing back at him. 'I love you, Ricco. That is all that matters, isn't it?'

'Yes! And it is so much more than I deserve, *cara mia!*'

His head came down and his mouth took hers again in a drugging kiss which left no room for the sudden fear Anna felt at what he might have meant. Suddenly the world shrank to this, to the feel of Riccardo's mouth on hers, the desire building inside them both. This was something she remembered so well, a part of the past which was even more important now, in the uncertain present.

She wove her fingers through his hair, drawing his head down further, needing this reassurance so desperately. Her lips parted to allow the entry of his tongue, and she shuddered at the exquisite sensations as it stroked against hers. Riccardo's hand slid down her throat, tracing the delicate lines of her collarbone, then moved down further to brush her breasts, straining against the confines of the cotton nightgown. Anna gasped, her body arching towards his caressing hand, her body throbbing.

'Ricco!'

He smiled against her mouth, repeating the slow caress until she was writhing beneath his touch. He drew back then, and slowly slid the straps of the gown off her shoulders, his face going rigid as he studied the delicate curves laid bare to his gaze.

'So beautiful, *innamorata*, so very, very beautiful. . .'

His deep voice was rough with desire, his passion held in check by the slenderest thread, and Anna shuddered as she realised it. She reached up and slowly unfastened the buttons down the front of his shirt, her cool hands slipping inside to trace the warm, hard muscles beneath, her eyes holding his until he groaned deeply. He closed his eyes, his heart thundering beneath her palms as she smoothed her hands down his strong chest, then slid them around his waist as she sat up and pressed herself against him.

She gasped softly as her breasts flattened against the hard wall of his chest, shocked by the wild flare of sensation she felt. His skin was burning hot against the coolness of hers, rough where the hair grew in a thick patch across his breastbone in delicious contrast to her smoothness; never before had Anna been so conscious of the differences between their two bodies, nor revelled in them so completely!

'Witch! You drive me wild with desire for you—but you always have, Anna! Always and for ever I shall feel this need to have you . . .!'

He pushed her back against the pillows, his hands moving over her as he stripped the nightgown from her. Anna closed her eyes, giving herself up to the heady sensations. Riccardo played her body like a delicate instrument, and the music he wrought was heavenly.

He shed his own clothes in a fever of impatience, dropping them carelessly where they fell, his skin burning to the touch as he lay beside her and drew her to him so that she could feel the throbbing thrust of his desire. Cradling her face between his hands, he kissed her tenderly, his mouth so gentle that Anna felt tears start to her eyes. He kissed them away, his eyes the palest glimmer of silver as they held hers in a look which was both tender and fierce.

'We have everything here that we shall ever need!'

He didn't wait for her to answer, his mouth hungry as it claimed hers once more.

Anna responded to him with an equal hunger, wanting to feel the heat of passion melting away the last of her uncertainty.

But later, as the long, hot waves faded, she knew with an aching heart that it wasn't enough. The doubts were still there. For both Riccardo's sake and her own she had to find out the truth. She had to be able to look at Riccardo and *know* that Sofia had been lying!

Had Riccardo discovered that she had gone yet?

Anna sat on the edge of the seat as the taxi sped through Milan's early-morning traffic. Riccardo had been sleeping when she had crept out of the villa to drive to Pisa airport. She could only imagine what his reaction would be when he woke to find her missing after last night!

She had been driven to do this, but she knew with a sense of cold dread that if Sofia had been lying then she herself would be responsible for the damage to her marriage.

The taxi dropped her outside the house. Anna let herself in, her footsteps echoing hollowly as she crossed the huge hall with its black and white tiled floor. She opened the drawing room door and got a shock when she saw the dust sheets shrouding the furniture. She passed from room to room, but they were all the same. The house must have been closed up for some while—longer than a short stay in England followed by the weeks in Tuscany seemed to denote—and her heart started to hammer.

How long had the house been closed up? Since. . . since she had left Riccardo almost a year ago?

On leaden legs she walked to the study. The key lay here, she knew that with a certainty which was laughable after all the uncertainty recently, yet her mind remained infuriatingly blank as she opened the door and looked around. On a sudden impulse, Anna dragged the dust-sheets off the furniture then stood and willed herself to remember, but nothing came to mind. Had she really gone through all this to be met only by blankness?

She sank down onto the chair behind the desk as cold waves of anticlimax rolled over her, then gasped when the telephone suddenly rang. It seemed to echo around the room and inside her head, as though there were a dozen telephones ringing, and slowly, with no fuss, no fanfare, the door in her mind swung open at last. . .

'Then rest assured I shall not let him down, Signora Falcone. I shall leave immediately.'

'But what is it about? Do you have any idea?' Her own voice, shrill with alarm, tinged with fear.

Eduardo Rossi hesitated. 'I am sure that it is nothing Riccardo and I cannot sort out. Leave it to me, *signora*, and do not distress yourself too much.'

Anna replaced the receiver. How could she help but worry when Riccardo was at the police station? What was going on? She started to slip the notebook back into the drawer, then stopped when she saw the photograph. What was it doing there? Who was it of?

She lifted it out and gasped with horror. It was of Riccardo, a formal portrait taken several years before. Anna recognised him at once, despite the huge black slash of ink across his face. Her mind recoiled from the viciousness of such desecration even while the questions ran through her mind. Who had done it, and why?

She turned it over, wondering if she would find a clue there. Riccardo often wrote inscriptions on the back of photographs; she had one of him herself, that Nell had taken that day he had followed her down to the river. Anna carried it everywhere and could recall Riccardo's tender amusement when he had seen it. He had taken it and laughingly written a dedication on the back, but his eyes had been loving as he had handed it back to her. . .

She forced the sweet memory aside, recognising the flowing handwriting on this photo at once as Riccardo's, reading what it said: "From your loving son, Riccardo". Underneath another hand had written something that Anna found impossible to make out, but for some reason she felt driven to find out more about what it meant.

It was purely with that aim that Anna took the folders out of the desk. The photo had been amongst them, so would they hold the answer? She opened the top one and stared down at the pile of newspaper cuttings. They were yellowing with age, the corners brittle; she sorted through them and tried to make out a word here and there, but it was only when she came to the last one that she had any inkling of what she had uncovered.

Her hand stilled as she stared at the grainy image of a young Riccardo standing alone by a funeral cortège. The headline was in big bold type, the words surprisingly written in English: THE KING IS DEAD, LONG LIVE THE KING! And underneath... underneath three brief lines stating that the funeral of Alessandro Falcone, head of one of the most influential Mafia families, had taken place that day in the presence of his son, Riccardo, who was now heir to the Mafia throne!

'No!' The denial was instinctive, but her mind spun, lifting small incidents from the past which had held little importance before yet now suddenly took on a new meaning: the respect with which people treated Riccardo, which wasn't respect but fear; the life of luxury they led, which came from the profits of crimes too vile to contemplate; Riccardo's reluctance to let her meet his family . . .! Suddenly it all made sense. The man she was married to, the man she loved, was the head of a Mafia family which dealt in death and drugs and every kind of perversion known!

Anna scrambled to her feet, upsetting the chair in her haste. She stared at the litter of cuttings, the photograph with its ugly ink mark, then turned and ran from the room. But she couldn't run from the truth as she finally knew it. With a choked sob she raced up the stairs, stumbling as tears blinded her. She reached for the handrail but the polished wood slid through her fingers, and suddenly she was falling, falling. . .

'Anna! Are you there? Anna!'

The memories splintered like glass, the shards of the past almost too painful now. Anna sat where she was, listening to Riccardo's rapid footsteps coming closer, and wondered how she was going to bear the agony a second time.

The door swung open and suddenly there he was, his face set, his silver eyes blazing with emotion. That he was furiously angry she didn't doubt, yet it didn't touch her. Was this what dying felt like? she wondered numbly. This coldness, this total bleakness in the soul?

'So I guessed correctly, Anna. I could not believe it when I woke and found you had gone. But then it struck me just where you might be. Did it not occur to you that I would be worried? Or is it too much to expect my wife to show me that much consideration?'

'What worried you most, though, Riccardo?' she asked hollowly. 'Where I was or what I might discover? Was your concern based on your fear of me finding out a second time what you have gone to such lengths to keep from me?'

'And what exactly have you discovered, Anna?' His voice was soft as he came further into the room, but it wasn't through gentleness. Anna had a feeling that he was restraining himself with an effort, and she shuddered at the thought. She had never feared Riccardo, but then she had never really known him, or what he was capable of. Now she had a good idea.

He must have sensed her thoughts, because he swore roughly, his eyes blazing as he came across the room and stopped before the desk. He had obviously left the villa in a rush, because he hadn't stopped to dress with his customary care, had simply dragged on black jeans and a thin black cashmere sweater. His jaw was shadowed with beard and it made him look even more the stranger—tough and uncompromising as he stood there staring at her with eyes like molten steel.

'Do not look at me that way! It appears that you have your memory back, so remember—have I *ever* done anything to make you think you need feel afraid of me?'

Anna looked away from his angry face, wishing that she could feel something apart from this numbness. 'No, but then I always wanted to please you before, always accepted what you told me.'

'And now that has changed? *Si.* I realise that. Now you no longer wish to please me, otherwise you would not have run off like a thief in the night! Was it worth it, *cara mia*? Did you find what you wanted?' He laughed suddenly, his voice harsh and unforgiving. 'Does it please you that you think you have all the answers now?'

Anna got to her feet, her face paper-white, her eyes so dark that they looked almost black. 'It gives me no pleasure to find out what a fool I have been—not once but twice! How easily you duped me, Ricco. That is what hurts the most—that you used the fact that I love you to hide the truth of what you are from me!'

'And what exactly am I, Anna?' He smiled thinly. 'Is it not time that you actually came out and told me what you suspect? Even the last time you made your "discovery", *innamorata*, you never told me what it was that you believed I had done. You ran away rather than do so, but I think now you should say the words aloud when you have gone to so much trouble to find out what you have!'

How she hated to hear that cold sarcasm in his beautiful voice, to see that taunting challenge on his face. Didn't he care what she was going through right now? Maybe not. Maybe Sofia had been right, and he had wanted her back to make sure that she suffered for the insult she had dealt him by running away.

Anna lifted her head and met his mocking gaze, even though her heart was breaking. 'I found out that you are involved with the Mafia—as your father before you was. I don't think there is anything else I need to add, do you, Riccardo? That should sum it all up.'

'I see. And you found all this out from a few newspaper cuttings, if I remember correctly—*si*? That is your proof, *cara*?'

'Yes! That and other things! I remember it all now, Ricco! Everything that happened. The way you kept me away from your family, the way people always seemed so in awe of you. . .even that phone call to Eduardo Rossi.'

She laughed bitterly. 'There wasn't any attempt

to discredit your business, was there? The police found something in one of your consignments, but couldn't prove *you* were behind it! I imagine Rossi got you off the charges, then. That's probably what you pay him for, after all—to legitimise your dealings if the need arises. Although maybe he hasn't been able to perform miracles this time, and that's why you've had to turn to Patrick Grady for help! Is he on your payroll too, Riccardo? No, don't bother even answering that because now it all makes sense!'

'Does it? Perhaps to you, Anna, but to me it makes little. It makes me wonder why you are so ready to believe such things about me if you love me as you claim to do.'

His voice held a note which just for a moment almost made her weaken before she realised what was happening. 'No! You can't talk your way out of it again! You won't manage to convince me that I am wrong this time with a few soft words of reassurance, as you have been doing for the past few weeks! Oh, you are highly skilled at doing that, Riccardo, because I wanted to believe every word you told me. But it was all done with one purpose in mind: to keep the truth from me. Now no amount of sweet words will ever convince me that I am wrong.'

'Then there seems little I can say, Anna.' He turned and walked to the door, his back rigid. He paused to glance back at her, aloof and arrogant as he stood there for a moment. 'If you will excuse me, I shall go upstairs and change. Seeing as I am here, I shall go to the office for the rest of the day. I am sure that you will be glad to have the time alone to decide what you wish to do. We shall talk again when I get back.'

He closed the door behind him and Anna heard the sound of his footsteps crossing the hall. She stood where she was trembling with the aftermath of reaction. What would happen when Riccardo came back and they talked? He had made no attempt to deny his involvement with the Mafia, so if she had needed proof surely that was more than enough. Now all it came down to was a simple choice: could she live with Riccardo, knowing what he was?

She left the study, pausing only to drop her door keys onto the hall table, where Riccardo would be sure to see them, then let herself out of the front door and closed it behind her—closed it on her life as Riccardo Falcone's wife. But never again would she be able to close the door on these bitter, painful memories.

CHAPTER NINE

PALE English sunlight spilled across the tiny garden, yet Anna didn't see it, lost in her own world. Riccardo wouldn't follow her. She knew that. His pride was too great to allow him to come chasing after her, but that didn't stop her from wishing for the impossible to happen. Could they have worked things out if she had been prepared to compromise and accept him for what he was? She loved him so much, and being without him was almost more than she could bear, so that the thought was a bittersweet torment.

'Are you sure you'll be all right, Anna?'

Nell made no attempt to hide her concern as she appeared in the doorway. Anna knew that it had been a shock for her friend when she had turned up a few days before, but Nell had simply opened the door wide and hugged her. Anna had told her what little she had felt able to, left untold so much more, but Nell hadn't pried, hadn't even said "I told you so"—and she'd been entitled to. Nell had had her doubts about Riccardo right from the beginning, but Anna had been too in love to try to understand them. Maybe she should have tried harder, and spared herself this pain.

'Anna?'

'What? Oh, sorry. I was miles away.'

'And we both know where.' Nell glanced at her watch. She taught art at one of the local colleges and mornings were always a rush. 'I have to go. But the one thing I want to say is this: if you love Riccardo then talk to him.'

She held her hand up when Anna started to interrupt. 'No. Please listen. I know you're upset. You've been through a lot, what with losing the baby and the accident and whatever else you've carefully omitted telling me, but Riccardo loves you. That is something I never had any doubts about. And you love him—which has to be worth something in this world!'

She grinned suddenly. 'I'm in fine form this morning, aren't I? Pity help my poor students. I'll see you later, Anna, but think about what I've said, please.'

She was gone before Anna could answer, the noise of the door slamming sending a cloud of small birds winging from the trees. Anna watched their antics, wishing that she and Riccardo *could* simply sit down and talk things through and find a solution. But what solution could there be? Everything Riccardo stood for she abhorred.

There was a knock on the door. Anna started nervously and glanced outside, but it was only a delivery van with a parcel for Nell. Anna signed for it, then carried it into the hall and turned back to close the door. She stopped with her heart thundering when she saw the man standing outside on the step.

'Hello, Anna.'

For a moment she couldn't move, shocked by his

sudden appearance, then hurriedly she tried to close the door but he was too quick for her. He stepped into the hall, smiling thinly as he looked round with a lift of his dark brows.

'So, *cara*, this is where you choose to hide yourself away?'

She ignored the taunt, ignored the endearment, ignored the sudden surge of awareness which raced through her. . .as best she could! Her mind might reject everything Riccardo stood for, but her traitorous body yearned for him still!

'What do you want, Riccardo? Why have you come?'

'I should imagine that is obvious, Anna. I came because I want to speak to you.'

She gave a broken little laugh. 'What is there to say?'

'Much.' He moved towards her but she stepped aside, unable to cope with having him touch her right then. If Riccardo touched her, held her, kissed her, then it would be so easy to let him manipulate her into doing what he wanted!

'Then I suppose you had better come into the sitting room. Do you want coffee?' She led the way along the narrow hall, pausing to glance back at him, and felt the colour run into her pale face when she saw his expression.

'No, *cara*, I do not want coffee. That is not why I came, as well you know.' He caught her arm and drew her to him, his eyes glittering fiercely in the dim light. 'I cannot believe that you are prepared to throw away what we have because of some foolish misunderstanding!'

He tilted her face up to his, his breath warm and sweet on her mouth as he bent towards her, but at the very last second Anna turned her head so that the kiss missed her mouth.

'Don't! I won't let you manipulate me again like that! A few kisses won't erase what has happened, nor will they succeed in making me forget the reason why I left you.'

'No? But perhaps they would show you what is important. Or am I fooling myself into believing that your avowals of love meant anything?' He gave a harsh laugh, his face set into grim lines. 'That is the real truth, I think. Because if you had loved me then you would not have been so eager to believe the worst about me!'

'That isn't fair! You're making it out to be my fault, but if anyone is to blame then it is you! You lied to me right from the outset, didn't you, Ricco? About who you are and what you do. You knew very well that if I'd had an inkling of what you are involved in I would never have married you, but you carefully kept it all from me! Thank God that we lost the baby, because at least the child was spared the disgrace of knowing what his father is!'

She had wanted to hurt him as much as she was hurting, yet as soon as she'd said the words out loud Anna regretted them. Riccardo's grief over the loss of their child was as genuine as hers, now that she recalled it. It was tragic that it had happened—that fall down the stairs robbing her of the baby she had longed for even before she had known she was carrying it. Now she could recall so clearly the aching sense of loss she had felt, the emptiness—everything that Riccardo must have felt as well.

'I'm sorry. I had no right to say that,' she said softly.

'Why not, if that is how you feel?' He smiled thinly, but his eyes held a glitter of reawakened pain which cut into her as he let her go.

She touched his arm, then dropped her hand at once, shocked by the surge of raw emotion which ran through her, the need to touch him again and again. 'It isn't. I know that you would have loved our child and been a good father.'

'And still could be. We could have another child, *cara*.' His voice dropped, deep and slow and sweetly seductive in the silence. 'Come home with me, Anna, and we shall have the child we both long for.'

'You want me to come back after. . .after everything that has happened?' Her voice was husky with shock.

The thought of what he was asking was the sweetest kind of temptation. Riccardo's child. Just the thought filled her with a deep sense of longing. To have Riccardo's child was a dream which still lay deep in her heart even now.

He smiled at her with aching tenderness as he reached out and brushed the silky curls back from her temple. 'I want you, Anna. I always have. Without you life is not worth living. I simply exist from day to day. Come home with me and we shall make a wonderful life together—you and I and our children. All it needs is for you to say yes and we can put what has happened behind us.'

Could they? For a sweet moment Anna savoured the thought, and then reality returned. If Riccardo had even hinted that he would be willing to give up the life he led then she knew she would have agreed because it was what she wanted so much—but he hadn't.

Anna turned and walked blindly into the room, her back towards him as she went to the window, but even then he refused to release her from the torment.

'We could have it all, *cara mia*, everything we have both dreamed of. Look deep into your heart and you will see that.'

'Do you imagine it would be that easy?' She whirled to face him, her small body rigid against the pain. 'How can I simply ignore what you are and what you stand for? And could you live with me, knowing how I feel? It would tear us both apart, Riccardo! I can't understand why you don't see that—can't understand why you want me back, when all we would bring to one another is more heartache!'

His face closed up. 'I do not believe it would be like that, but it is a risk I am willing to take.'

'Why?' She laughed hollowly, feeling the tears pricking behind her lids. 'It seems masochistic to want to put yourself through that sort of torment!'

'Why do you think? Surely you know the answer to that question, Anna.'

His tone was suddenly hard, his expression

unreadable. What was he thinking, feeling? Anna had no idea, and it made her unsure. Suddenly, Sofia's taunting words came back to her. Anna hadn't given them any thought until now, when they struck her afresh. Riccardo had gone to great lengths to get her back before and was doing so again—why? Because he loved her, or for some other reason she had overlooked so far. . .?

Her heart lurched as she suddenly realised what the truth was. She raised pain-darkened eyes, her face stark and white.

'There was something else in your desk that day, wasn't there, Riccardo? Something you think I saw. . .' She swallowed down the knot in her throat, her voice little more than a whisper. 'Something which linked you to your Mafia dealings.'

'I have no idea what you are talking about! It seems to me, Anna, that you are starting to imagine things.' His voice grated—but was it anger or fear which put such hardness into it now? Anna had no idea, but her heart wept because suddenly she knew the truth—all of it.

'I'm not imagining anything, Ricco! The reason you want me back is because you are afraid of what I know and whom I might tell about it! I don't know anything about Italian law—whether the same principle exists there as it does in England, that a wife cannot be made to testify against her husband, but I suppose it is immaterial, really. Once you had me back under your spell then you knew I would never testify against you! And all that talk about a child. . .!'

Her voice broke on a sob, but she forced herself to carry on, hurting more than she had thought it possible to hurt. 'You refused to even consider the idea just a week or so ago. Why? Because you were afraid that it might trigger my memory if I found myself pregnant again?

'But of course my memory has come back, so the whole ball game has changed, hasn't it? Suggesting we have a baby is just another clever ploy to get me back, because you know how much I always longed to have your child! And it would serve as a double safeguard against me ever telling what I know—because how could I say anything against the father of my child? That has been the driving force all along, hasn't it? And yet the irony is that I saw nothing, Riccardo—nothing at all! Your secrets are perfectly safe!'

He stared at her for a long moment before he finally spoke. 'So, now you know it all, Anna.'

'Then you aren't. . .aren't going to deny it?' she whispered.

He gave a low laugh which held no hint of amusement. 'Deny it? Why should I do that when you have worked everything out so perfectly at last?'

Tears misted her eyes so that she didn't see him leaving—but then, she didn't need to. She felt it inside her, as though something had died. Riccardo left and took with him every precious dream she had ever had.

'Ricco! Ricco!' She whispered his name into the silence but Riccardo had gone.

* * *

The days dragged past after Riccardo's visit. Anna felt numbed by the pain of what had happened. She had been left with nothing now—no hopes, no illusions—and just coping with the emptiness was almost too difficult.

That Nell was worried about her was something she was aware of, and she tried to compensate for it by putting on a brave face when they were together. But Nell was at work all day, and the hours on her own seemed endless.

In an effort to rally herself, almost a week after Riccardo's visit, Anna caught the train into the city and spent the morning wandering aimlessly around the shops. She had to start making decisions about her future, but planning a future without Riccardo seemed more than she could cope with right then.

'Anna. . .it is you! I thought I recognised you, but wasn't sure. How are you?'

Anna stopped dead, staring at the man with blank eyes for a long moment, and heard him give a low, self-mocking laugh.

'Patrick Grady. . .remember? We met at the villa a few weeks ago.'

Her heart lurched painfully as she suddenly recalled who he was and how they had met. 'I. . . yes, of course. How are you, Mr Grady?'

'Fine, thank you. I must say it's a surprise to see you here. I was speaking to Riccardo only the other day, and he made no mention of coming to England.'

Anna blanched, turning away so that the man

couldn't see what she knew must be in her eyes—all the pain and anguish. 'Riccardo isn't with me.'

'I see.' There was a touch of speculation in Grady's voice now. He glanced around, then eased Anna to one side as a group of teenagers jostled them as they passed. 'How about a cup of coffee to get out of this crush?'

'I really don't think. . .'

'Please, Anna. It seems that you and Riccardo are both suffering from the same malady!'

Her heart jolted and she raised urgent eyes to him. 'Riccardo isn't ill, is he?'

He smiled thinly, taking her arm to steer her into a nearby coffee-shop. 'Let's just say that he isn't at his best right now—and I have a pretty fair idea of what is troubling him now that I've seen you.'

He ordered coffee for them both, then seated Anna at one of the tables by the window, his face very grave as he studied her for a moment. 'Didn't what we found out help in the end, then?'

Anna shook her head in confusion. 'I'm sorry, but I don't know what you mean.'

'About who was behind the attempts to discredit Riccardo?' He paused. 'He didn't tell you, did he?'

Anna could feel the shock running through her in spasms. 'It. . .it was true? Someone *did* try to harm Riccardo?'

'Of course.'

'But I thought—' She stopped, unable to admit what she had thought. She closed her eyes on a sudden surge of wonderous relief; Riccardo hadn't lied to her about that!

'I did warn him that day I came to the villa that he was playing with fire, but he wouldn't listen. Of course I understood why, even though I didn't agree with what he was doing.'

Patrick Grady's voice drew her attention again. Anna looked at him with a frown. 'Playing with fire. . . What do you mean?'

'Riccardo told me about your memory loss and what he was hoping for. I understood why he was so desperate to stop you remembering everything until he had things sorted out, but I warned him that it could all backfire and it seems that I was right. But if there is anything I can do to help, Anna, then I would be happy to.'

Anna looked away, her face devoid of colour.

'Why? Because you, too, are on Riccardo's payroll?'

'No. I don't work for Riccardo and never have—apart from helping him out recently when he needed it. The reason why I want to help you two resolve things is simply that in my view Riccardo Falcone is one of the best. It's an old-fashioned term nowadays, but above all else Riccardo is an honourable man. But you must know him better than anyone.'

'I thought I did! But it appears I was wrong.'

'Were you?' Grady waited while the waitress brought the coffee. 'It's easy to understand how confused you are, Anna. You've been through such a lot that it's bound to have had an effect. But look into your heart. It's the only way to ever find out what the truth is, believe me.'

He drank his coffee, then got up and dropped

some coins onto the table. 'I have to go, I'm afraid. But please do as I ask. I would hate to see you and Riccardo throwing away something special because of some silly misunderstanding.'

Anna sat at the table long after the man had left, still stunned by what she had just learned. Riccardo hadn't lied to her about the attempt to discredit his business. It had really happened—just as he had told her it had. It awoke the first small doubt. She had been wrong about that, so could she have been wrong about other things?

She got up from the table, the coffee untouched, her thoughts turned inwards as she searched for answers. But the trouble was that she knew far too little to find any. She and Ricco had fallen in love so quickly that they'd had little time to get to know one another. Their love had seemed enough, their passion a guarantee of happiness. They had lived in a fragile bubble of happiness, and when that had burst there had been no solid ground to fall back on.

Maybe there never would be. Maybe it was too late to go back and ask the same questions and find different answers. Maybe she was simply fooling herself into believing that there might be any, but she had to take that chance. She loved Riccardo, and if she had been wrong about him then she had to find it out!

The Villa Margherita lay serene and tranquil under a cloudless blue sky. Anna drew the rental car to a halt, feeling the warmth of the sun on her bare arms as she got out, but it did little to ease the chill from her body. All the way here on the plane, and then on the long drive, she had wondered what she would say to Riccardo, what he would reply, but now that she was here she had no clear idea how to go about it.

'*Signora*! I heard the car and when I saw you I could not believe my own eyes. I give thanks to the saints that you have come back!'

Anna spun round, shading her eyes against the glare, and spotted Maria hurrying towards her.

The woman's face was lined with concern, her agitation obvious, and Anna felt the chill turn to ice.

'What is it, Maria? Has something happened?'

'*Si, si.* Signor Falcone he has been. . .how you say?. . .*matto*!'

Anna struggled to make the translation, but failed. When Maria turned back to the house she followed her at a run, driven by the woman's urgency. She looked around the hall. 'Where is Signor Falcone?'

Maria's eyes lifted to the ceiling. 'Up the stairs. He has been there for the past few days. I have taken his meals up but he has not eaten them. I did not know what to do, who I must tell. . .'

Anna patted her arm, her heart thundering. 'It isn't your fault, Maria. I am sure you have done all you can. I. . . I shall just go up and see what is wrong.'

She could feel Maria's eyes following her as she made her way up the stairs. She turned along the landing, her hand trembling as she tried the handle on the bedroom door, but it was locked. She knocked lightly on the wooden panels, her heart hammering, her voice sounding unnatural to her own ears. 'Riccardo. . .are you there? It's me.'

The silence seemed to echo back at her before a harsh laugh came through the door. 'And who might that be? My loving wife? The woman who swore in front of God to honour and cherish me?' His voice sobered suddenly, so flat and emotionless that Anna felt her heart twist in anguish. 'Go away, Anna. I do not wish to see you or speak to you. I do not think we have anything worth saying.'

It took every scrap of strength she possessed, but she made herself stand there. 'But I want to speak to you, Riccardo. That is why I came—to see you, speak to you, to. . .to try and sort this out.'

The door swung back on its hinges, and Anna gasped at the sight of Riccardo standing before her. There was a heavy shadow of stubble along his jaw and his clothes were rumpled, as though he hadn't bothered to change them for some time, but the silver eyes were staring at her so coldly and forcefully that she almost backed away.

He gave a harsh laugh, obviously amused by her reaction. 'Do you not like what you see now that you see it, Anna? Perhaps you should take that as a warning that you will not like what you hear if you insist on talking.'

He was goading her, quite deliberately trying to drive her away, and suddenly she felt her temper surge to life. She pushed past him, slamming the door behind her, her own eyes glittering back at him. 'Perhaps I won't! But that's for me to decide, isn't it? It isn't for you to decide for me. It isn't up to you, Riccardo Falcone, to feed me the scraps you want me to know. I want to hear it all—good and bad!'

'But I thought that was the trouble, *cara*, the fact that you had discovered that there is no good in me, just bad. Surely that was what sent you running away from me the first time—and the last.'

He shrugged, as though it was of little importance what she believed. Anna would have been convinced of his indifference if she hadn't caught a glimpse of the agony etched on his face as he turned and walked across the room. It was enough to make her want to stay and force the truth out of him!

'Yes, it was what made me run away. But I've come back, Riccardo, because I realised that I should have stayed and made you explain everything to me.'

His eyes flashed as he turned to stare arrogantly at her. 'I should not need to explain, Anna. My wife should trust me enough to know the truth without it needing to be stated!'

That stung so much that she felt tears in her eyes, but she blinked them away. 'Maybe you're right. Maybe I should have known you well enough to know the truth, but the trouble was, Riccardo, we neither of us knew one another, did we?'

She gave a laugh which held a world of pain and saw his mouth compress. It was such a small sign but it meant so much; it told her that even through his anger Riccardo hated to see her hurting. He loved her; suddenly there wasn't a single doubt about that in her mind!

She crossed the room and stopped before him. The sun was streaming through the open shutters and it set fire to the soft curls clustered on her head, lit her delicate features so that they held an almost ethereal radiance. She heard the soft sigh Riccardo gave, her name uttered in a tone of such anguish that she yearned to comfort him.

'We met and fell in love so quickly that we didn't have time to learn anything about one another, did we, Ricco? It seemed that our love was enough and that we didn't need anything more than that, but it was foolish to build our future on such fragile ground.' She paused, giving him the chance to say something, but he remained silent so she carried on, voicing aloud everything she'd been thinking on the journey there.

'I was very young when we met, and inexperienced. I thought that love was all we needed, but no one can live their life in a vacuum. 'The world and its ugliness was bound to intrude at some point and it did that night you asked me to phone Eduardo Rossi. I. . . I found that photograph in the drawer quite by chance, and then, needing to understand what it meant, looked further and. . .'

She couldn't go on but Riccardo continued for her, his deep voice flat. 'And found the newspaper cuttings. When I came home from taking you to the hospital the next morning they were still on the desk, and I knew then that you had seen them, read them. I even guessed what interpretation you might have put on them, but I told myself that you loved me and that it would make no difference.' He laughed bitterly. 'What a fool I was, Anna!'

'That isn't fair! What did you expect me to think? You had deliberately kept from me who you really were, made sure that I never met any of your family, so it was only natural that I should fear the worst.'

'Perhaps, but did you never once consider that you might have made a mistake, that things were not what they seemed? Did loving me, living with me, being my wife make no difference, Anna?' His fingers bit into her bare arms as he suddenly reached for her and held her, his silver eyes blazing. 'Was it so easy to believe a few scraps of paper and so hard to believe in me, your husband?'

'Are you saying that you aren't. . .aren't. . . involved with the Mafia, Riccardo?' Her voice was hoarse, and she bit her lip to contain the sudden desperation.

He let her go so suddenly that she staggered—distancing himself both physically and mentally from her, Anna felt. 'I am not saying anything. I should not need to. You should know in your own heart who the man you married is. If you do not then there is little anyone can say to convince you.'

He shrugged indifferently and started to turn away again. Anna felt her temper surge to life, pain and anguish sending it soaring. 'Damn you, Riccardo Falcone! Damn you for your arrogance, for your stupid pride. You would rather stand aside and let me walk out of your life for good rather than tell me the truth, wouldn't you?

'You say that you love me, but it's a strange kind of love that dictates you would rather lose me than compromise! Maybe I should know the answers without needing to ask the questions, but unlike you, Riccardo, I am only human. I have doubts and fears and I need reassurance! But if you would rather stand there and watch me walk away again, then go ahead and do so!'

She swung round on her heel and marched to the door, her heart aching, her temper burning. He really was the most insufferable, arrogant. . .!

'Wait! Where do you think you are going? Come back here.'

Anna's eyebrows arched. No please, no thank you, no polite request—just that curt order which he expected her to obey! She glanced round, her face haughty with disdain, her slender body poised gracefully in the doorway. 'I have said all I came to say. If there is anything to add then you come and find me and tell me, Riccardo. That is if you manage not to trip up over that enormous great pride of yours!'

She was out of the door and down the stairs in seconds, Riccardo's angry roar echoing after her.

Slipping into the car, Anna gunned the engine and shot away in a shower of gravel, watching through the mirror as Riccardo came to a halt at the top of the steps. From the expression on his face he wasn't at all pleased by her departure, but that couldn't be helped. What happened next was up to him.

Her hands clenched on the steering wheel as she

guided the car along the twisting road, her heart suddenly lighter than it had felt in days. She knew no more now than when she had first arrived, so it seemed premature to let herself start hoping for what might never be. But then sometimes, if one wished long enough and hard enough, miracles did happen. . .

CHAPTER TEN

THE river flowed past, the silver water sluggish as it made its way between the rolling green fields. Anna lay on the grassy bank, wondering if she was a fool to remain there. Hope had given way to despair as the time passed. Riccardo wasn't coming after her!

She closed her eyes on a sudden spasm of pain, then opened them again as a shadow fell over her. For a moment she couldn't seem to move, thinking, speaking, even breathing suspended, then Riccardo sat down beside her and leant across and kissed her and the world spun back to life.

She kissed him back just as hungrily, just as urgently as he was kissing her—her mouth clinging, her hands lifting to wrap around his neck and hold him. His body was warm and hard and so achingly familiar that it felt like a homecoming having him in her arms, feeling him holding her in his. And in that moment Anna realised that, no matter what, she needed Riccardo in order to be whole.

'Darling. . .*caro*. . .' She whispered the soft endearments to him as he pressed her back against the damp, warm grass and kept her there with the weight of his powerful body, and felt the shudder which ran through him almost as though it was pain he felt, not pleasure. He drew back a fraction, his eyes glittering with determination as they met hers.

'I shall never let you go again, Anna! Never!'

'Why? Because you are afraid of what I know?' She had to challenge him even now, needing the reassurance of hearing the words although she knew the answer in her heart before he gave it.

'No! That was never a consideration. I do not understand how you ever imagined such a thing. I love you, Anna. As God is my witness, that is why I wanted you back and why I want you now!'

His urgency made her shudder, her heart shaking her with its beat. 'And I love you, Riccardo. I shall never leave you again because I need you, darling. I need to be with you for ever.'

This kiss was just as hungry as the first, but far too short. Anna's senses were whirling as Riccardo suddenly sat up. She sat up too, trying to control the swift flow of emotions and concentrate, but it was hard to concentrate on anything except Riccardo.

She glanced at him, seeing the tautness of his jaw, the thinness of his lips. He had obviously showered and changed because his hair was still wet, his clothes fresh, his face smoothly shaven, and she felt her senses stir with that deep awareness she always felt around him.

He turned and looked at her, his silvery eyes knowing as he saw in her face how she felt—but then, Riccardo had always known, the same as she had always known how he felt about her. They loved each other, and that was something worth fighting for.

'Tell me, Ricco. Tell me it all, please. We have

come too close to losing everything to make more mistakes.'

'You are right, Anna. I should have explained it all sooner, but I was afraid to tell you in case I lost you. How bitterly ironic that it almost happened anyhow!' He laughed harshly and her heart stopped. Was he admitting that he was involved with the Mafia?

She asked herself the question and suddenly she knew the answer, couldn't understand how she hadn't known it before. Riccardo, this man she loved with all her heart, could never be involved in anything so ugly.

She put her hand on his arm in a gesture of implicit trust. 'I know I made a mistake, Ricco. I know that no matter what I saw that night, and what I believed then, you could never be involved in something so awful.'

He covered her hand with his. 'How do you know, Anna? Only a short while ago you still believed it. So why have you changed your mind?'

'Because I know you.' She touched a hand to her breast. 'My *heart* knows you, *caro*, and my heart tells me that you could not be mixed up in something so evil.'

He raised her hand to his mouth, his lips warm as they touched her skin. 'I have wanted to hear you say that for so long, Anna. That is what hurt the most—that you could believe me capable of being involved in such business—yet even through the hurt I could understand why you should think so. I should have told you before we married, but I wanted you so much and I was so afraid that you would never marry me if you knew my past.'

'Then it's time we cleared it all up. I... I don't think I could bear to go through this another time.'

Her tone reflected her pain and Riccardo winced, but he made no attempt to take her into his arms, as though he was steeling himself to tell her the whole story first. 'My family was—is involved with the Mafia. You understood that much from the things you saw in the desk. I was thirteen before I realised just who my father was and what he stood for, and sixteen when I made my decision never to become involved in his world.'

He shrugged, but the old pain lay starkly on his face and Anna felt her heart ache. 'Your father took it badly?'

'*Si.* It was to him the greatest dishonour that his son should turn his back on our way of life, but I could not have lived with myself if I had allowed him to draw me in. I told him that I would never work for the Family. And that very day I left his house and never went back there again, not even to see my mother—because when he was alive my father forbade it, and after he died she would do nothing to go against his wishes.'

He paused, as though even now he found it painful to speak about that time. 'That photograph you found in the desk was sent back to me by my father. On it he had written that he had no son. I kept it as a reminder, but I never regretted the decision I made.'

'Oh, Ricco! How awful for you. You were so

young. . .' She could have wept at the thought of how he must have felt.

He smiled gently, kissing her lovingly on the lips. 'You have a tender heart, Anna. It is one of the things I love most about you. However, I survived because I was determined to. I set myself up in business with some money my mother sent me without my father's knowledge. It must have been as hard for her as for me, because I was her only child. It was in deference to her that my father ordered that the rest of the Family leave me alone—because there was much ill-feeling at the time. They had the power, if they chose to use it, to bring about my downfall.'

He shrugged, as though dismissive of that thought, but Anna had read things about the intricate powerful web of Mafia families and the revenge they could wreak on any who crossed them. She shivered at the thought.

'Now times are changing, and others are deciding that they do not wish to follow in the old ways. The fact that I have never once revealed anything I know about the Family has gone in my favour, and they have left me alone over the years and allowed me to build my business up to what it is today.' He tilted her face and stared deep into her eyes. 'Everything I own I have worked for. Nothing is the result of crime but of legitimate business dealings. I want you to believe that, Anna. It is the truth.'

'I do believe it. I really do! But it can't have been easy for you.'

'No. I worked hard. And always going against me

was the fact of who I was, that I was the son of Alessandro Falcone. It affected people's perception of me, and I cannot lie and say that it did not do so. It opened some doors for me and shut others, but I could not change who I was. I am the product of my heritage even though I have chosen to turn my back on it—and you must understand that, *cara*. I am and shall always be the son of a powerful Mafia figure, and the world will judge me accordingly because of it.'

'It doesn't matter what people think! I know what you are, Ricco! I only wish I had realised sooner.'

'It was hard for you, Anna. As you say, we knew so little about one another. I blame myself, because I understood so much better than you that we cannot shake off our past just by wishing to do so. That night I asked you to contact Eduardo Rossi is proof of how the past intrudes on the present. I told you that I had been having problems with my business—minor irritations—but that day was different, what happened far more sinister.' He paused, his face set.

'What happened?' Anna probed, needing to know.

'A shipment was brought into port, and, following information they had received, the customs officers opened it and discovered a small amount of drugs.'

'Drugs!' Her voice reflected first horror then disbelief. 'But they couldn't possibly have believed you were involved in drug smuggling, Riccardo!'

He laughed out loud. 'Thank you, darling. If I had

needed any reassurance that you believe in me then that would be more than enough.'

She joined in the laughter, but her green eyes still held a glow of indignation on his behalf. 'But who was behind it, Riccardo?' She stopped, gasping at the thought. 'The Mafia?'

'That is what the police thought at first. They believed that I was using my business as a front for them. It took Eduardo's skill and the fact that they had no solid evidence to connect me to what had happened to convince them in the end.'

'Do you know who was responsible?' Anna gasped. 'Was that what Patrick Grady was trying to find out for you?'

'Yes. The police found nothing, and as there were no further incidents they let it drop after a while. But I was not satisfied.' He shrugged, but his expression was severe. 'At first I, too, wondered if it had something to do with the Family—but why then, after all those years? And the more I thought about it the less sense it made.'

'Why? What do you mean?'

'It is well known that the Mafia is involved in drugs—but in such small quantities? No, it would not be worth their while. And then there were the other things which had happened—all those silly little incidents. It was not their way. Whilst it was a relief to realise they were not behind what had happened, I still needed to know who was. It was a deliberate attempt to discredit me and my business, and I could not allow it to go unchallenged.'

'And you found out, didn't you?' She laughed

when she saw his surprise. 'I saw Patrick Grady in London the other day, and he mentioned something about it. It made me realise how wrong I had been, and that you had been telling me the truth. And if I could be mistaken about that then how many other mistakes might I have made?'

'Then I shall be for ever in Patrick's debt.' He kissed her lingeringly, smiling when he heard the soft moan she gave—although he, too, was breathing faster than he had been, Anna noticed with satisfaction. 'It appears that Sofia was the culprit.'

'Sofia?' She stared at Riccardo in shock before suddenly it all made sense. 'Because she was angry at the way you had broken off your relationship with her to be with me?'

'*Si.* Is there not a saying about a woman scorned? Sofia was behind it all, but I did not start to realise it until that night we met her at the restaurant. I saw then that her anger had turned to hatred, and it made me look more carefully at what had gone on. But by then I was desperate to find out the truth, you see.'

There was such anguish in his voice that Anna caught his hand and held it. 'Why?'

'Because I wanted to prove to you that I was not involved in any criminal acts.' He turned her hand palm up and pressed a kiss to the centre. 'I had lost you once through my own foolish pride, but I was desperate not to lose you a second time.

'That night when we got back to the villa I almost told you everything, but I was afraid you would not believe me. Then, when we made love, I thought—

hoped—that it meant you were starting to trust me again. I made up my mind that I would tell you everything you had forgotten the next morning and trust in our love to see us through, but. . .'

'But the next morning I had gone to Milan,' she finished softly. 'I'm so sorry, Ricco. I had to go! Sofia had told me that I had left you, and you cannot imagine how I felt, learning such a thing. I didn't want to believe her, but I couldn't disprove it because I couldn't remember. It was such a bitter blow, because that night we had been closer than ever. Then all the doubts came back, all the uncertainties, and I knew that I had to know the truth for both our sakes.'

'I can understand that, *cara*, but you cannot imagine how *I* felt when I discovered you had gone again. It was just like the first time, and such a bitter blow when I had been so hopeful that we would work things out. I told myself that you could not love me if you were unable to trust me.'

'I never stopped loving you, Riccardo. It was just all so confusing. All I could think was that I must go to Milan and see if that helped. And suddenly I remembered everything. It was as though my worst nightmare had come true.'

'Anna, my darling, it was my fault. I should have told you. . .'

She kissed him softly. 'It was both our faults and the result of circumstance too. Looking back now, I realise that perhaps if we had spoken when I came back from the hospital after losing the baby we could have avoided much of this heartache. But we were both struggling with our grief. We became more and more distant, until I couldn't stand it any longer and left.'

'Where did you go? I tried so hard to find you but no one seemed to know where you were, not even your friend Nell.'

Anna laughed shakily at his wryness. 'I didn't tell her so she wouldn't be forced into telling lies for me. I went to Birmingham and got a job there, but it was a dreadful time. I missed you so much, wanted to see you so badly—but I was afraid.'

'Of me? Anna!'

She hurried to reassure him. 'No! Never of you, but of myself. I knew that if I saw you again I would go back to you no matter what—if you would have me. I told myself it was better that way, but I was lying to myself. It was like being half alive without you.

'I moved down to London, hoping that a change of scene would help, but it made no difference. Every day was a nightmare, every night even worse. Then I had the accident and. . .well, you know the rest better than I do.'

'*Si.* I was in England on business at the time. It was purely by chance that one of the newspapers carried a small article on me.' His hand tightened, his face stark at the memory. 'You cannot imagine how I felt! I had given up all hope of seeing you again, then suddenly that phone call. . .'

He drew her to him, holding her so close that she could feel the heavy beat of his heart against her breast. 'I did not dare hope that it was true at first, that you would be there when I arrived, and then I saw you lying so pale in that bed.'

He kissed her hard and passionately before he gently set her from him again, although he kept hold of her hands, as though he couldn't bear to lose all contact. 'I sat in that room by your bed and all I could think of was how we had first met, here by the river.'

Anna smiled. 'That was what I dreamt about. It was so odd because until then I hadn't dreamt of anything, but that day suddenly my head was full of pictures. Then I woke up and saw you. Isn't that strange?'

He shook his head. 'No, *cara*. I think some greater force than we might ever understand was working for us. Our love made our two minds link on that day, and because of it you came back to me.'

'But not all of my memory returned, Riccardo. Why didn't you try to help me remember?'

'Because I was still afraid. It seemed to me that I had been given a second chance but that I could lose it again so quickly. I did not want you to remember until I could prove to you without any doubt that I was not involved in what you believed. Every day I woke terrified that it would be the day you remembered, that I would look into your eyes and see loathing there, not love.' He held her gaze. 'It had nothing to do with what you might have seen in my desk, Anna. There was nothing there to see because I have never been involved with the Mafia. I wanted you back only because I love you.'

She smiled shakily, not doubting his sincerity.

'You said once that you wanted me to fall in love with you again.'

'*Si.* That is the truth. The more you loved me the easier it would be, I thought, for you to believe in me.' He gave a deep laugh, brushing her soft mouth with a light kiss.

'You cannot imagine what lengths I went to, how desperate I was to stop you remembering too soon! I was even afraid that making love to you would unlock your mind, but in the end I could not resist your beauty—yet I was haunted by the thought of how you might hate me for it later when you did remember. That was why I did not want us to have a child too soon. I would not trap you into staying with me. You had to want to do so, freely.'

'I could never hate you! I wanted you to love me, Riccardo, because only in your arms did I feel safe. When we made love the world seemed right; it was when we were apart that the doubts crept in.'

She paused, suddenly aware of what he had said, and frowned. 'What do you mean about the lengths you went to to stop me remembering?' She gasped as realisation dawned. 'The telephone! Did you do something to it, Ricco?'

He smiled at her shocked face. 'The telephone did not work because of the storm—that much was true. But that was before we arrived at the villa.' He shrugged, a wealth of arrogance in the gesture. 'I simply arranged for the line to be disconnected after we got there.'

'Why, you. . .you. . .!' Words escaped her; she could only glare at him from stormy green eyes, but when he ran his finger across her mouth she couldn't hide the shiver which quickened her body, and she knew that Riccardo had seen it.

'*Si, cara.* I am most probably all the things you are trying to say, but I did it because I could not take the chance of you telephoning anyone and discovering what I was so desperate to keep from you.' He stared at her, sincerity in every taut line of his face. 'Maybe it was partly selfishness, but I wanted to protect you from the past until I had enough answers to convince you of how wrong you had been. It was never my intention to hurt you.'

'Oh, Ricco!' She gave a tender little laugh. 'So what else did you do? Confess!'

He gave her a teasing smile. 'Shall I tell you, Anna? I would not like to arouse your wicked temper even more.'

She glared into his taunting silver eyes. 'If you don't tell me it all, Riccardo Falcone, you will regret it! Rest assured of that!'

'Ah, well, in that case I have no choice. I arranged for Carla and Guido to go away on holiday for a while, just in case either of them said anything to remind you of the time you had forgotten.'

'You really are the most scheming, conniving, double. . .!'

'But you love me, *si*?' He laughed gently at her, his handsome face full of tender adoration, and Anna felt her heart melt.

'I love you. . .*si*.'

He framed her face between his hands, staring deep into her eyes. 'I know what I did was wrong. I knew it even before we left England. Dr Lewis was very suspicious, I could tell, but what I did, Anna, I did out of love. I was desperate to have everything straight by the time you regained all your memory, because I could not bear the thought of losing you again.'

'I understand. I think that if the positions had been reversed then I might have been tempted to do the same.'

'I hope the occasion will never arise. I promise you, Anna, that I shall never do anything to bring dishonour upon you or the family I hope we shall have.'

'I love you, Riccardo Falcone. I am proud and happy to bear your name because I know you for what you are.' She smiled up at him. 'And the children we have will be proud of their father too.'

His silver eyes glittered with emotion as he swept her into his arms and held her tightly to his heart. '*Cara*. . .I love you with my whole heart. I shall spend my life trying to live up to your belief in me.'

'Just love me, Ricco,' she whispered, lifting her mouth for his kiss. 'That will be enough. . .'

EPILOGUE

LITTLE Paolo Falcone was baptised in the same church where his parents had married. Afterwards the party returned to the Villa Margherita to enjoy the lavish spread Carla had prepared and set out in the gardens, so that they could take advantage of the warm spring weather.

Anna watched her son being carefully carried down the garden in his godmother's arms, and smiled with utter contentment. She was so lucky to have all this when she had come so close to losing everything.

'Happy, my darling?'

Riccardo slid his arms around her waist and drew her back to rest against him while he pressed a light kiss to her temple.

'Yes! Happier than I can tell you.' She turned in his arms, her green eyes adoring him. 'I love you so much, Ricco.'

'As I love you, Anna.'

His voice deepened, his silver eyes ablaze as they met hers, and Anna felt her senses stir. She gave a small laugh, reading his mind so easily. 'What a pity we have guests to entertain, darling. . .'

He joined in her teasing laughter, his eyes sliding past her to the small group gathered on the lawns with the baby at the centre of all the attention. 'I do not think our guests need any entertaining right now. They seem quite happy.'

Anna glanced round, smiling as she watched Nell carefully settling baby Paolo in Patrick Grady's arms.

The choice of godparents had been simple—Nell standing as godmother for their child, with Patrick Grady and Eduardo Rossi as his godfathers. All three had played their part in bringing about this moment, and Anna had had no hesitation in asking them to perform the task.

Now, as she watched Nell and Patrick standing so close together, she wondered if perhaps she had done them a favour!

Her eyes glittered with warm amusement as she turned back to Riccardo. 'Do I detect a hint of something between Nell and Patrick, do you think? They seem to be getting along extremely well.'

Riccardo laughed throatily, tilting her chin to kiss her lightly, then let his mouth linger a moment longer when he felt her instant response. 'Perhaps it is simply that you want everyone to be as happy as we are, *cara*? But it proves my point that we shall not be missed for a little while. Come.'

He drew her with him into the house, leading her to the study and closing the door behind them before taking her into his arms. The kiss was everything Anna could have wished for, full of the love which filled each and every day of their lives now. She kissed him back just as hungrily, needing to show him how she felt. The baby had been a seal on their happiness—the beginning of a new, wonderful time in their lives.

'Thank you, *cara.*' Riccardo's voice was husky with desire, his silver eyes full of flames as they held hers. 'You have given me so much that I once thought I had lost.'

Tears glistened in Anna's eyes as she reached up to brush his mouth with a tender kiss. 'We have given each other so much, Ricco. We are so lucky to have one another, and to be blessed with Paolo as well.'

He smiled wickedly, running his hand lightly down her spine in a caress which made her body tingle. '*Si*, and this is just the beginning. We shall have other children, Anna, brothers and sisters for little Paolo. . .in time.'

Anna laughed, leaning back in his arms as she stared into his laughing face and saw the wicked gleam in his eyes. 'Mmm, and if you have your way those brothers and sisters won't be a long time coming! You, Riccardo Falcone, are a wicked, scheming man to play upon my susceptibilities this way! You know how hard I find it to resist you.'

'Yes, and it is something I take great delight in, *cara.*' He bent and kissed her lingeringly, his mouth hardening with desire before he set her from him and walked to the desk. Opening the top drawer, he took a small velvet-covered box from it, then came back and held it out to her.

Anna took it hesitantly and opened the lid, gasping as she saw the exquisite diamond and emerald ring.

'Ricco, it's gorgeous! But why. . .?'

He took the ring from the box and caught her hand, slipping it onto her finger next to her wedding band before pressing his mouth to her knuckles. Because I love you, Anna. Because I want you to wear this and always remember that.'

Anna lifted her arms and slid her hands around his neck to draw his head down. 'It's beautiful, Ricco. Thank you. But I don't need anything to remind me of that.' She gave a soft little laugh, feeling the way his body hardened against hers and drawing out the moment a while longer in sweet anticipation of what was to come. 'There is nothing wrong with my memory now. I remember only too clearly how you always make me feel!'

'And I have no intention of ever letting you forget it, Anna!'

His mouth claimed hers, and sweet anticipation became even sweeter reality.

One to Another

A year's supply of Mills & Boon® novels— absolutely FREE!

Would you like to win a year's supply of heartwarming and passionate romances? Well, you can and they're FREE! Simply complete the missing word competition below and send it to us by 28th February 1997. The first 5 correct entries picked after the closing date will win a year's supply of Mills & Boon romance novels (six books every month—worth over £150). What could be easier?

PAPER	B	A	C	K		**WARDS**
ARM						MAN
PAIN						ON
SHOE						TOP
FIRE						MAT
WAIST						HANGER
BED						BOX
BACK						AGE
RAIN						FALL
CHOPPING						ROOM

Please turn over for details of how to enter ☞

How to enter...

There are ten missing words in our grid overleaf. Each of the missing words must connect up with the words on either side to make a new word—e.g. PAPER-BACK-WARDS. As you find each one, write it in the space provided, we've done the first one for you!

When you have found all the words, don't forget to fill in your name and address in the space provided below and pop this page into an envelope (you don't even need a stamp) and post it today. Hurry—competition ends 28th February 1997.

Mills & Boon® One to Another
FREEPOST
Croydon
Surrey
CR9 3WZ

Are you a Reader Service Subscriber? Yes ❑ No ❑

Ms/Mrs/Miss/Mr ______________________________

Address ______________________________

____

______________________ Postcode ______________

One application per household.

You may be mailed with other offers from other reputable companies as a result of this application. If you would prefer not to receive such offers, please tick box. ❑

C496
A

MPS MAILING PREFERENCE SERVICE

DMA